INNERLAND

Mark Holden

-CHAPTER ONE-
Judgment Day

    I raced through the front door and threw my report card in with a pile of old mail on the coffee table. After grabbing a quick snack, I bolted up the stairs, past the landing, and into the safety of my room. Even though today had been one of the most horrible on record, I had made a terrific a discovery as I meandered home: Captain Amazing, issue number eighteen!
    As excited as I now felt, it was odd that my day hadn't started out very well; Dad had been on my case, as usual.
    "Jeff. Why aren't you doing better in school?" Dad, of course. I hadn't even finished my breakfast-bowl of King Munchies yet.
    "I don't know, Dad. If I did, I would probably do better, don't you think?" Maybe my response was a little too sullen, but I was running late for school as it was. Besides, I was tired of the constant interrogation. Dad was not amused by my tone.
    "Don't get smart, young man," he admonished me between bites of his granola cereal. "You know, it might help if you spent less time with your comics, and more time with your school work," he added, as he finished eating and got up to take his bowl to the sink.
    "Yea, but the comics are what got me turned on to reading in the first place!" I protested.
    "I didn't say that reading comics was bad, Jeff," he retorted, "And I really don't see a problem with your interest with reading them, any more than I see a problem with your constant fascination with drawing. All I'm asking you to do is to strike a balance. You know, do a little studying now and then, along with reading comics and sketching super-heroes? Vary your life a little, Son. It's like eating pizza all the time," he teased as he ruffled my hair.
    "But I like pizza!" I protested.
    "So do I, Jeff. But not for breakfast, lunch… and dinner!"
    I had to think about his last comment a little, because I really like pizza. As I reflected on how bloated I felt from the pizza we'd gorged ourselves on last night, and the thought of eating the cold, clammy remnants for breakfast, I kind of began to see his point.
    "OK, Dad," I relented, "I will try and do better today."

"That's all I've ever asked, Son," he said with a smile, as he gripped my shoulder and steeled me with his cold, gray eyes. Sometimes, when I look into my dad's face I swear he's a lot older than forty.

I really did mean my commitment to Dad. I had high hopes to do better. My intentions were sincere, as they always had been before. However, a bad day can do a lot to spoil the noblest of intentions.

The first bomb came when I had to stay after the bell ended second hour class. Mr. Measer, my math teacher, was on my case about me not getting my work done.

"This homework situation is getting out of hand, Mr. Ransford."

I wanted out of there as quickly as I could manage. It is never a comfortable situation to be confronted by Mr. M. He doesn't let anything slide, and I swear half of his students, including myself, think they might get arrested if they cross him.

"It's only one assignment, Mr. Measer." A lame excuse, I know, but the best I could come up with.

"Only one assignment, that's true," he stated, as he continued to block my exit from the room, "But the day before yesterday it was one more." He closed the classroom door, and walked slowly over to his desk. Picking up his grade book, he continued, "And let's see... Hmmm... Oh yes. And only three assignments missed last week... Two the week before that... Oh, here's a good one; only a single missed assignment four weeks ago! That must be a sort of record..."

Before he could continue, I interrupted him. "Mr. Measer, I know I haven't been doing well, but I will try harder. Really."

At this point, Mr. Measer strode back over to me, and locked my gaze with his. He spoke in low, measured tones. "Mr. Ransford. I pride myself in letting my students exercise their free will. However, when a student misuses that free will, that student chooses to give up certain privileges that he used to enjoy. That student is you, Jeffrey Ransford." I frowned; my sentence was about to be passed. He continued on, as unemotional as ever, my judge and jury. "Beginning today, and through next quarter, you will not be allowed to go home until you finish the current assignment, and make progress towards making up your fifteen missing assignments from this term. I cleared this with your father about an hour ago."

"You called my dad... at work?"

"Let me finish," Mr. M demanded, his features turning grim. "You will report to Counselor Weshy's office to serve detention for one hour daily. You are dismissed."

"Detention? Mr. Measer, that's not fair!" I protested. Up until this point, Mr. M had been one of my favorite teachers. Even if I didn't understand most of what he taught, he always had neat ideas, and I enjoyed listening to his stories about all the jobs he had held before he became a teacher.

"It is not a subject which is open for discussion at this point, Mr. Ransford," he replied coolly.

"But-," I began.

"I said you were dismissed!" It was the first time Mr. M had ever raised his voice with me. I slunk out of his room to an empty hallway.

The rest of my day followed pretty much the same pattern. I was late for my next class, of course. Even though it was just P.E. Coach Nakitani wasn't too impressed with me being tardy: I got to do four laps as a consequence. At lunch the cooks served broccoli surprise. Yuck. I went hungry. And then, last period, we received report cards. I did get two A's: one in Art, and the other in P.E. I knew Dad well enough, however, to know he would be unhappy with the D's and F's that made up the remainder of my scores for the third quarter.

I was a pretty dejected fellow as I sauntered home that night. That is, until I happened to stop by 'Ken's Burger Stand and Comic Shop.' Captain Amazing is enough to brighten up any day, especially when I found the climax issue to a story I had been waiting several months for. Even though I was really hungry, it was good that I had saved my lunch money. I eagerly bought the comic.

A half hour later, when I finally entered my bedroom and let my book-bag slump to the floor, I flopped down on my bed and ever so carefully slid my recent purchase out of its plastic bag. It was hard to be careful; I was anxious to find out how the Zorg battle ended that had been going on for the past year, ever since issue number six. Thrilled as I was, I somehow managed to keep my new comic in good condition as I delicately laid it open on my bedspread.

Vibrant colors jumped out of the page at me! Figures and poses of familiar characters were more lifelike than I remembered. The opening frame took up an entire page; Captain Amazing struck a majestic stance with a laser pistol still smoldering in his right hand.

Cap's left foot thrust below the bottom edge of the frame so that it looked like he would walk right off of the page! No doubt about it, Big John Basaldua was the best when it came to illustrating comic books. Alpha Comics would always have a loyal customer in me as long as they continued to employ him as an artist. I had never met him, but I admired his skill; John was almost as big a hero to me as Captain A!

After flipping through a few pages, admiring more of the vivid artwork, I began to lose myself in the flow of the story. I could barely believe it had been nearly four weeks since I had left Captain A at the mercy of Queen Zorinda. It only took him a page and a half to escape from her evil clutches and get his hyper-ship out of space-dock. Imagine, the mightiest ruler in the universe leaving only one guard to protect Captain A's ship, the Space Skimmer: the bad guys are always so dumb in comics! I wished some of my teachers at school were as easily foiled as Queen Zorinda's minions. Soon Cap was cruising back to the planet Terrain with the peace module he had stolen from the Zorg fortress. Trust me, the module was crucial to finally ending this story. You wouldn't believe all of the adventures Captain A had to go through to get the silly thing back!

I sat down, and began to lose myself in the flow of the story:

> *Captain Amazing pulled his ship out of hyperspace. Waiting for him were two Zorg battle cruisers! "I have gotten out of worse situations," he confidently thought. "Even though the Zorgites are great warriors on the ground, they think two-dimensionally. They don't do so well in the three-dimensions of space."*
>
> *Captain A maneuvered the Space Skimmer between the horizontal-plane of his attackers. The maddened Zorgs piloted their ships to each side of the Skimmer with weapons locked. Cap waited 'til the last possible moment, and then decelerated his ship (causing his relative altitude to diminish). His would be assassins obliterated one another without Cap having fired a single shot! "Now, on to the planet Terrain to rescue the peace loving Terrainians from Zorg oppression!"*

This was it! The climax to a story I had been waiting an entire year to see resolved. I took a breath, and continued reading.

Cap knew, even as his ship came into orbit around the planet, that nothing could stop him from his appointed mission. Nothing could distract him from...

"Jeffrey. We need to talk."

Uh oh. Jeffrey. My full name... not just Jeff. Dad's stern voice broke the spell, which the comic book story had begun to weave upon me. I should have been more careful than to have left my report card on the coffee table. I reluctantly turned away from the comic I was reading.

Typically Friday was the one weekday I could relax as I moved into the weekend. Most of my teachers had made this Friday the exception. Looked as though my dad, Thomas Ransford, was determined to keep on with the break in tradition.

"Could we make it later Dad? I just got the latest issue of Captain Amazing. They're finally starting the war with the Zorgs that they've been leading up to for six mon-"

"Jeffrey," interrupted my father, "We have to talk. Now."

"I don't mean to be rude Dad," I countered, as I stood up, taking my new comic book into hand, "But I've had a really bad day at school, I'm just getting into this comic and want some time to myself for-"

Suddenly a storm of paper filled my vision, and my eyes were assaulted by a kaleidoscope of color! Plastic casings separated from comics, magazines hit the floor, the wall, and the ceiling; in the middle of this man-made tempest stood my father!

I stumbled back into my chair, disbelief etched on my features. This was my property Dad was destroying! I had gathered each issue with painstaking care over the course of years. As I frequently enjoyed each magazine, over and over again, I recalled my own history. Cosmic Man number four lay crumpled in the corner; I had gotten that one when my buddy John and I went to Magic-Land Mall two summers ago. The premiere issue of The Interlopers lay bent under my chair, missing its cover. It had been one of the first comics I had purchased with my allowance after Mom died when I was only seven.

My comics... My comics! I had worked six years to build my collection. It hadn't always been easy to find the issues I wanted in this stupid little Oregon town. I had gone without lunch most days so I could afford to purchase the issues I wanted with the money I'd saved. Dad would never talk with me about Mom's death, or anything else, so I sought out this now much preferred company. My comic collection had become my companions in the last several years. Dad had just destroyed my friends!

As my father turned to face me, I sat helpless, my body racked with silent rage. Captain Amazing number eighteen slid from my trembling hand, all but forgotten.

"I am... sorry..." Dad began, somewhat reluctantly. His face flushed red. "But now that I have your attention, we need to talk."

I looked at Dad then, as he towered above me, heard the formation of his words, but I didn't really listen. I could not believe what he had just done to me.

-CHAPTER TWO-
Escape Into Imagination

After a few minutes of hearing Dad's lecture my mind wandered. I'd heard Dad's sermon before anyway; this was his 'Settle Down to Reality' discourse.

He began to rehearse what I already knew too well: that I was failing almost all of my classes, except for art and P.E.

In art I had maintained an 'A' average throughout middle school. My talent in detail could probably be attributed to all the comics I spent time looking at. That, and artists like John Basaldua that I tried to emulate. I drew pictures and doodles constantly, when I didn't have my nose in a comic, that is. I often missed notes I should be taking in class, but always got some great character sketches, or portraits of the other students.

P.E? Getting an 'A' was easy with Coach Nakitani. He demanded a lot from his students, but he also made his classes more interesting than most other teachers made theirs. Though I was lousy with most sports, Coach made me want to do my best, so I usually gave him a good effort. The self-defense unit had been my favorite because instead of struggling against other players I could compete against myself. I had gotten to where I could control my body movement after just a few weeks.

Science? It was interesting, and I even got along well with Miss Devesek, who I found to be rather cute, for a teacher. However, the math got in my way. As for other subjects, to be honest, I didn't even feel like trying anymore. I had a feeling that most of the teachers thought I was dumb; I had begun to believe them, and they seemed to have given up on me.

I'd committed to Dad and several of my teachers (including the school counselor) that I would work really hard to improve my grades this quarter. It was an easy commitment to make. Heck, I'd given it on several different occasions. I really did mean my promises too. Well, until Alpha Comics had come out with four new super heroes, each with their own monthly magazine! Even my best commitments couldn't compete with my devotion to comics. No matter how much I meant my commitments at the time, I had aspirations to illustrate comics. I saw no use for most of the stupid classes that Mrs. Weshey insisted I take.

Dad continued to vent his angry feelings concerning my latest progress report, and my mind continued to wander. As I glanced about the room, my eye caught sight of a single pinhole left pressed into the wall above my desk. I had tried putting a calendar up last year. That had been a mistake! Our home, located near the Northern-Pacific Coast, had been in our family for generations, since before many of the pioneers had migrated west. Dad had thrown a fit when he saw the calendar. He never let me put posters up, never allowed any holes in the wall, not even a pinhole. I guess he really cared about this old house. Anyway, Dad made me take the calendar down. I thought it funny now, after the fit he'd thrown, that Dad had never patched the hole.

That solitary pinhole continued to hold my attention… I glanced at it more and more as Dad continued to lecture me. That little prompt was all it took. My imagination took over and my thoughts wandered away from the fight with Dad.

Conflict, especially with my father, is not the thing I deal best with. Mrs. Weshy, the school counselor, says my active imagination is a safety valve. She claims it is my way of dealing with unpleasant situations; a way of escaping my father when his reality gets a little too 'real' for me to handle. I think of it as 'changing channels;' from the boring nightly news to an action-packed movie. My daydreams are usually triggered by a simple object I notice in my immediate surroundings. I start thinking up a comic book type story, and while I'm letting my imagination create new stories I remember to occasionally shake my head and mumble, "Yes, Dad," so I don't make my father any more angry than he already is.

My escape-ploy must work pretty well because after lecturing me, Dad usually gets a satisfied look on his face, like he just taught me the purpose of life or something. Many times I can't really remember what the problem was to begin with, but I usually have some great ideas for drawings, and sometimes even a good story idea or two. I save my ideas because I will illustrate comics one day; it is my dream.

I admit that the way I handle these situations may be kind of mean, but I also figure Dad and I come through an awkward situation both getting something we want. He gets to give his lectures, which he must enjoy due to the frequency I hear them. I get entertained by some really wonderful adventures of the imagination, and store up ideas for my future.

Sometimes the object that triggers a story might be a stapler, a paper clip, or get this: even a whisker on my dad's chin. Once, during one of his 'you should be more responsible' lectures, I came up with a really great idea for a spy comic book. In my story, the secret agent smuggles classified microfilm inside of a tiny canister the size of a whisker. All he has to do is wear a day's growth of beard on his face. The enemies in my story never figure out that my unshaven secret agent is smuggling top-secret plans out of their country via his facial hairs. He sneaks the plans right under his nose as well as theirs. Anyway, I thought it was a good story. I even illustrated some great pictures, none of which were hung on my wall, of course.

This time, instead of facial hairs or paper clips, the imagination-spark was a tiny pinhole in my wall. My story idea was this: a scientist figures out how to shrink down to the height of a pinhole at will because of a neat little micro-chip which he has surgically implanted into his brain. Could come in real handy if he accidentally got caught by the bad guys; Nobody would see him escape after he had shrunk.

I closed my eyes for a moment, while I continued to daydream about 'Mini-Man', remembering to occasionally say, "Yeah, Dad," and nod my head, my dad continued on his vehement tirade. "You need to buckle down and get your head out of the clouds, Jeffrey, and settle down to..."

Then, quite suddenly, I could no longer hear my dad. I opened my eyes to find I was no longer sitting in front of him either! Instead, I was standing in a circular tunnel about as wide as it was tall (which was a little taller that my five foot frame.) Ahead of me was semi-darkness, a little luminescent. For some reason, the walls of the cavern let off a subtle glow. Behind me was much lighter. Naturally I turned around to see where I was (or what I was daydreaming about.)

The sight that I beheld surprised me enough to make me stumble and nearly lose a precarious footing!

Standing a kilometer above and below me was my dad! He was still in the standing position I remembered, with his hand and arm gesturing threateningly towards the chair I had occupied a split-second before. The chair was now empty. Dad's mouth was opened in a half syllable, as if he were trying to finish a word he had begun to form. He didn't need to. I had heard that lecture lots of times before. "Buckle down, get your head out of the clouds, and settle down to ... reality." I began to form a silent response, as I had many times before, "What about dreams Dad? Don't dreams play a part in all this 'real world' stuff somehow? Wasn't it someone's dreams that brought us to this wonderful reality of computers, space travel, and video games that we enjoy today? Didn't it take someone dreaming about things being different?" I wondered if Dad's dreams had died when Mom's body had. And then, as I had many times before, I almost felt sorry for him.

But not this time… Not quite. Still lingered the resentment I had felt as a seven-year-old boy towards a father who would not even bother with a funeral for his mother. Still fresh in my memory was the mass destruction he had just wrought upon my collection of comic books. The same collection I had labored hard to gather for what seemed like most of my life. I thought about how particular I had been in selecting just the right copy of each issue. I reflected on the time taken to carefully seal each comic in its own plastic bag. And then I recalled how he had thoughtlessly swept my comics onto the floor of my room. All I had room left in my heart for was complete, livid, anger... and hatred! I felt no room in my soul to pity anybody who tried to destroy my dreams, not even my father. His aspirations died six years before, but mine... mine were just beginning!

Back away from that ledge, I thought as I turned around. Looks like a long drop to the bottom.

As I mentioned, deeper into the pinhole cave, the walls put off their own light. The surface of the rock was saturated with pale, lime-colored goo that gave off a dull phosphorescent glow. I'll just walk a little deeper and find out what's making the light. This seemed like a good idea. I could shake my head and say, "Yeah Dad," a lot when I snapped out of the dream. He wouldn't know I hadn't really been listening. Like I suspected of my teachers, he may not even care. Dad and I were pretty good at talking about what we were feeling, without either of us ever really listening to what the other one was saying.

But right then I didn't want to think any more about Dad, about school, about loss, or about guilt. My escape of imagination was what mattered, and I wanted to enjoy it. I briefly reflected on the problems of the day, staring at the giant, inert form of my father, and I decided that I would enjoy my fantasy for as long as I could make it last. I could always hear the homework lecture, but this... this was living!

Now... About the source of that light...

I turned around and walked forward, down the inside of the lengthy tube. I was anxious to see what my imagination would concoct for me as I followed the glowing source to the far end of the 'pinhole' tunnel.

As I walked, it occurred to me again and again what a 'real' feeling this daydream held for me. It was more intense, more vivid than any dream I remembered experiencing previously. I felt as if I were really stepping along the floor of a gently sloping tunnel. I sensed the pressure of my body pushing down against the soles of my shoes. I noted the closeness of the walls, felt the gentle pull of air as it passed deeper into the passage before me. *Wouldn't it be wild*, I thought, *if this daydream were really happening?*

I have read many stories about characters in books acting hesitantly when faced with new or unusual situations. I never could identify with that type of person. I always dreamed of being the actor in an unusual story of my own. Despite the constant feelings of 'realness,' I knew I was only imagining my surroundings, although I wished it were otherwise. Even though it was just my imagination, I was going exploring!

-CHAPTER THREE-
Of Pinholes and Passages

Leaving the fight with Dad behind me, I hoped to enjoy my fantasy world for as long as I could. I leisurely walked along the tunnel, using the faint light source in the far distance as a guide. I walked for a long time down this 'pinhole' cave. After awhile I finally came to an offshoot that veered right of the tunnel I was traveling and down. From this heading a faint green glow emanated. I was curious to understand the goo that made the tunnel glow, so I groped on in this direction. I climbed and tumbled down a level or two of passages. Even in the dim half-light I could tell the tunnel was fairly regular in shape. The corridor was still shaped like the inside of a tube or a barrel. Carved from solid rock, it must have taken someone forever to dig the tunnel.

Stopping to rest after I had been walking for what seemed about thirty minutes, I caught my breath. It hadn't been an especially long walk so far, but the curving nature of the floor (as well as the sides and ceiling) made it difficult to traverse. It was like trying to walk lengthwise down the inside of a large oil drum.

Eventually I came upon the portions of the cave that glowed. They were immediately to my right and left. It seemed curious to me that the tunnel didn't glow from the ceiling or the walkway. Anyway, leaning against the slanting wall, I rubbed my hand hard against the side of the cavern. When I drew my fingers back they glowed with some of the same greenish hue of the cave wall, though not as intense. Maybe the glow-in-the-dark stuff smeared on the walls had been rubbed in or even painted on. I couldn't guess beyond that, not knowing what it was.

After another brief respite I decided to continue with my explorations. A few more minutes in the passageway and I began to come across offshoots to this glowing tunnel. I continued to follow the one I was in however as it seemed like the most recent; the glow from the walls was brighter than that of connecting tunnels.

Soon the rounded floor along which I was walking gave way to more of a flat, rough-hewn surface. This appeared to have been cut with tools, as the floor hadn't been smoothed out like the first tunnels I had traveled. I negotiated several small rectangular shaped compartments, and finally came to a door which was squared on the bottom and rounding at the top. It appeared to have been made from some type of wood, yet of a grain and color that I did not recognize. Feeling an irrepressible curiosity I pushed it open.

On the other side of the door stood a serious looking fellow, thin but muscular, maybe nineteen or twenty years old. His skin was pale; not sickly looking, just pale. His hair was jet black and shoulder length. The light skin and deep black hair reminded me for a moment of my mother. He wore no shirt, but a kind of beige leather kilt with subtle green tones in the hide. Deep blue and green embellishments decorated the hem. He wheeled about as I came though the door, confusion and anger gripping his features as he quickly pulled a Roman style short sword from a sheath tied to his thigh. The sword was pointed directly at me!

"Krok! You are but a boy. What are you doing here?" He demanded, as the set of his jaw remained rigid. He continued to hold the sword between us.

I answered as best I could, given the circumstances. "Don't worry, I'm just having a crazy daydream!"

My answer, unfortunately, didn't seem to put him at ease.

"My name is Jeff," I offered, hesitantly extending my hand in friendship.

The sword remained balanced horizontally between us.

"I won't hurt you," I continued. "I have been wandering through these tunnels behind me. When I found a door I was curious, so I opened it." As I finished my explanation I pointed over my shoulder, back the way I had come.

His sudden reaction of laughter caught me off guard. Now it was my turn to wear a confused expression.

"Your clothes do look like something an Otherworlder might wear, little boy. Though even I do not imagine them wearing such outlandish costumes as that. Krok! Who put you up to this? Jured? Oh! I owe him dearly for this!"

Besides not knowing what he was talking about I was insulted: jeans, basketball shoes, and a Captain Amazing tee shirt were not what I would refer to as an 'outlandish costume.' Heck, I had even done the silkscreen for this shirt myself in Mrs. Tistry's art class last fall! Where I came from these were considered a bit more stylish than a man in women's clothing!

"Better come along with me, little boy," the prehistoric adolescent in a skirt continued. "I feel some mirth as a result of your joke, but the Ancients of West Reach might not think it was very funny for a child to have been playing around in the sacred tunnels of the Otherworlder. The Ancients have waited many cycles for the reappearance of the Deliverer, and they might take exception to your mucking about out here."

I was beginning to dislike this teenage body builder. His continued emphasis on the word little was starting to wear on me. Granted he was my superior physically, but he didn't seem to be that much older than me. Even so, I finally ventured a question. "What is your name anyway?"

"Tabob," he said between chuckles, "Tabob-Guard. Son of the Ancient named Vocata." He then motioned for me to follow him deeper into the catacombs of tunneling. These were not as well lit, so Tabob grabbed a sort of glowing torch from a wall sconce to light our way. The torch was not lit by fire. I thought it was more like a flashlight because of the glowing end and the beam of light it threw off. However, I didn't see how anyone could get batteries inside a wooden stick, which was what this appeared to be. I made a mental note to examine it more closely when I got the chance.

Approximately thirty minutes later I was begging for a break because of the growing stiffness in my legs. I was tired and my traveling companion wasn't particularly talkative. I decided that this daydream was getting out of hand, even as an escape ploy. I tried to concentrate on the confrontation with my dad in order to terminate my 'mind story.' This had been what I had done to yank myself out of previous daydreams, so I was more than a little concerned that it didn't work this time. It occurred to me then that this might be a full-fledged dream from which I was not yet ready to awaken. Oh well, I thought, It can't be too bad as long as I don't fall off a cliff and hit bottom before I wake up.

When experiencing other 'sleeping' dreams I had realized at the time that I was dreaming. Given this, the fact that I knew I was dreaming now didn't seem all that odd to me. What I found peculiar about this particular dream was the fact that I couldn't remember anything happening after my fight with Dad the night before. Our 'discussion' must have really made an impression on me, I thought as I fell into step again behind the Neanderthal in a dress. I didn't remember feeling so physically tired in a dream before either. I hoped at least I would be well rested when I finally woke up.

After what seemed hours of vigorous trudging through blackened tunnels, and feeling personally exhausted, we finally came to a huge wooden door. The door was similar in design to the first I had come through, though much larger. My arrival at the previous door now seemed hours ago. Tabob led me cautiously through the doorway and quickly slammed the door shut with a resounding thud. After glancing suspiciously around several times, he opened a panel carved from the rock on the outside of the door. Reaching inside he appeared to trip a lever (I couldn't see exactly what he was doing at the time) that secured the massive door. He tugged on the door two or three times to test its fastness and closed the hidden panel. We continued on, this time striding down hundreds of broad carved steps that led up to the door. Scattered all about on this side of the doorway, lining the walls, were thousands of dead and wilted flowers, bowls of grain, a variety of small knives and bows, and piles of colorful folded clothing and material.

A short jaunt later, after negotiating the cluttered stairs, we came to what appeared to be the outskirts of a tiny town bustling with many people, most with features similar to Tabob. I noticed a few different colors of hair (brown and grey) but all had the same pale skin. Most of the inhabitants wore clothing similar to Tabob's, except the women were dressed a bit more modestly. Many people greeted Tabob in a friendly manner like they all knew him, only to then give me a perplexed look and suppress a giggle.

The buildings surrounding me looked like Scandinavian or Russian hamlets of the medieval period that I had seen pictures of, but with one strange difference: the entire village was contained within a single immense cavern- It was all underground! I continued to be fascinated as we emerged into another cavern, the largest I had yet seen.

Stretching to the edge of sight before and to the side of me were lush old growth forests of pine and fir trees. The effect was the feel that I was in a gently sloping forest stretching away from me; rather like being inside of a bowl. The twilight showed to me colors and details like I had noted only after rainstorms back home. The spicy scent of the greenery rejuvenated me after my expedition through the stale tunnels. An intricate system of rivers and canals meandered endlessly across the face of the scene before me. Even a few small lakes dotted the landscape like sapphires set in jade. More houses could be seen grouped in the distance. We appeared to be following a path that would bring us to the biggest conglomeration of buildings visible. Towering in an irregular dome over the whole scene was the cavern ceiling, probably a half-kilometer above. Even with the return of the faint green glow of the walls, I felt a sudden anxiety to be above ground in the open air. I felt some relief when a light breeze kicked up bringing fresh air and waking me up a bit. The wind came from my immediate right, though I was not certain of the cardinal directions. The draft pulled the smoke from a few chimneys and ushered it off into the distance, presumably to another cavern. I also felt some reassurance in reminding myself that this was merely a dream; yet more vivid than any fantasy previously experienced.

Tabob led me to a lavish looking three-story home near the center of the town. Intricate woodworking and multiple colors were embedded in the designs on the posts surrounding the doorways. The designs and colors on the exterior of the house matched those on the hem of Tabob's skirt. Both were different from neighboring dwellings.

Turning, he addressed me. "I appreciate your joke, little boy, and the companionship during our journey. But we are home in West Reach." Laughing again, he continued, "I will tell Jured you played your joke well. Now. You ought to go home to your family. Your mother is probably wondering where you are."

At the mention of my mother, and considering the possibility of being alone in this weird dream, I suddenly felt more like a little boy than I wanted to admit.

"I don't have a mother... Anymore." I admitted reluctantly.

"I am truly sorry," Tabob managed awkwardly, his expression quickly changing. "I didn't mean to... Where do you stay?" He finally stammered.

"On the other side of the tunnels we just walked through," I replied, motioning with my thumb and feeling suddenly exhausted at the thought of having to walk back though all of those sloping tunnels.

At my casual mention of this, Tabob grew ashen faced, quickly excused himself, and withdrew into the recesses of the doorway.

Now what? I thought. *I told him that I had come through the tunnels when I first met him. Why is he acting so surprised all of a sudden?*

Feeling tired anew, beyond anything I remember, I sat down against a multi-colored porch support and closed my eyes for a few moments. *This is definitely different. I don't remember falling asleep within a dream before*, I thought as my eyes rolled closed and my world turned slowly black.

* * *

"You should have known, Tabob." An elderly male voice reprimanded softly and slowly as I stirred into wakefulness. "He may have been the reason you were sent to stand as sentinel at the Great Door this Eighth Cycle."

It seemed to be much later in the day when I finally opened my eyes. Even when I thought this, it seemed funny to me because I knew we were still in a cavern. Yet the constant glow, which surrounded us, seemed dimmer, almost like twilight.

I stared hard at this ancient man stooped over me, his wrinkled face spread wide in a grin of pleasure that seemed foreign to his wizened features. He was somewhat pale, like Tabob. His hair appeared to have at one time been almost as black as his younger companion's, yet now was streaked with a varied assortment of grey and white. He seemed familiar to me. *Almost*, it struck me as odd even as I thought to myself, *Almost what I might look like as an old man.*

"My name is Vocata," spoke the ancient one slowly as he held my gaze, and took hold of my right hand. "Vocata the Ancient. I have waited for a great many cycles to finally meet you. Welcome to Innerland's West Reach, Jeffrey."

-CHAPTER FOUR-
Vocata, the Ancient

I simply sat there leaning against the post, my mouth agape. I could form no words for a reply.

"I am very glad to finally meet you, Jeffrey," repeated the old man staring deeply into my eyes. "I had begun to think my life might be over before I finally got to make your acquaintance. I am pleased that it is not. Seeing you now, it was worth all the cycles of waiting," rambled the old man, oblivious to my shocked, open-mouthed stare.

How does he know me? I've never met him before! I thought in alarm. *Wait a second*, I finally realized, *What's the big deal about the old guy knowing my first name? This is a dream, it comes from my brain. So my thoughts are controlling what is happening.* (At least that's what the school counselor had told me.) *If all of this is coming from my mind, why am I surprised that this imaginary guy knows my name? He should! Especially since he's a product of my imagination...* Even talking to myself logically, I felt little in the way of reassurance. I was still nervous that this dream character Vocata knew my name was Jeffrey.

I suddenly realized that Vocata and Tabob were looking at me pretty intensely, both wearing expressions of genuine concern.

"Is everything well with you, Jeffrey?" queried the old guy, while still holding tightly to my hand.

"Everything's great," I said. *And you guys are just a weird dream*, I thought.

"No we are not," Vocata sternly asserted as he looked more searchingly into my eyes.

"What?" Tabob and I said simultaneously.

"Please don't interrupt me, Tabob," Vocata admonished the youth. "There is more being said than you can hear, Son. Please stay alert, and learn."

Tabob shamefacedly backed up a step, and silently sulked.

"Now," Vocata continued as he turned back toward me, "I assure you, Jeffrey, this is all very real, and you are not dreaming," he declared emphasizing his word choices. "It is strange that you seem to think you are somehow imagining our world. No one has come from Otherworld without knowing that a purpose forced them to transfer into this reality. Very strange indeed."

You're the strange one, old geezer, I thought, as Vocata continued to hold my gaze.

"Jeffrey, I know you hold a higher position of authority than me, having come from Otherworld and all. Still, 'old geezer,' whatever it means, is not the proper title to address me by. Ancient One would be more appropriate, being as that is my title. Even Vocata, my name, would be preferable, and acceptable since I consider you to be a friend."

I couldn't believe this guy; he was reading my thoughts!

Tabob stayed in the background, now holding a gnarled hand over an ever-increasing grin. If Vocata really was his dad, he could have been remembering father's lectures wherein Vocata knew exactly what he was thinking, and if he were lying. *I'm sure glad my dad couldn't tell what I was thinking during his lectures to me*, I thought with relief.

"Oh, but he could," replied Vocata.

By this time Tabob was laughing out loud, despite a stern glance from his aged father.

Knock it off! I shouted in my mind, becoming increasingly frustrated. *And if you can read my mind, why don't you know I prefer being called Jeff, not Jeffrey?*

"Very well… Jeff," vocalized Vocata, "But it will take much more time to converse using speech rather than thought."

I returned Vocata's searching gaze for a moment. *Are you still reading my mind, Vocata? Ancient One? Old Geezer!*

Vocata returned my gaze neutrally.

"Your thoughts are not now open to me, Jeff. You may trust me," he maintained. "I am a man of integrity, and I do not at this time know your thoughts."

Even though I didn't know him, instinct told me I could trust this guy. It just felt right.

Pulling me up by my hand that he still held clasped in his, with a strength belying his rickety frame, he continued the conversation.

"Like I before mentioned, I don't know why you felt this were a sort of imagining or a dreaming. I believe from all I have been taught that you should have known your purpose prior to coming here. It is the perspective I have had since I was a boy, learning at my father's knee."

He steeled me with an extremely serious expression, and then continued.

"Do you believe me when I tell you that you being in our world is real, and is not at all a dream?"

I nodded yes. I thought, *No!*

Vocata was not convinced.

"Tell me, Jeff," he continued, "Have you ever before, in a dream, felt a hand in yours as real as mine feels?"

I winced as the old man tightened his grip on my hand!

"Have you ever before felt such great fatigue, during a dream journey, that you fell asleep within that dream? Jeff... You are here. Many of us have waited long for you to come. It just doesn't make sense for you to be here now. I feel somehow that overcoming your disbelief will get us closer to understanding why you have been elected to come at this time, and not another."

Reluctantly, I began to believe this old fellow. Partly because I had worked so hard to convince myself I was dreaming in the first place. And partly because, well, like I mentioned before, it just felt like I could trust this guy.

Vocata released my hand, yet continued to hold his extended towards me, with his palm up as if wanting something.

"Could I please see the Stone of Recognition, Jeff?" he asked.

As with many things so far since coming to this place, I had no idea what he was talking about. I felt like I did when I often forgot my homework in Mr. Measer's math class: a little guilty, a little confused. I guess my feelings must have shown in the expression on my face.

"You don't have it, do you..." It was more of a statement than a question.

I shook my head negatively.

Tabob looked shocked.

Vocata slowly nodded his head from side to side, then said, "My, my... but this does complicate matters."

Vocata stood there for a moment as if deep in thought. I was beginning to feel a more keen guilt, probably about his disappointment in me not having what he wanted.

After a few awkward moments he turned, opened the door, and invited me inside his dwelling.

"We may as well eat while we figure this one out," Vocata said motioning me inside, a slight smile beginning to return to his lips. "You are welcome to stay with us, Jeff. For as long as you'd like, of course."

The suddenly acute hunger pangs deep in the pit of my stomach reaffirmed the belief I was starting to form that this was indeed, somehow, all very real.

* * *

If the outside of the house was extravagant, it was rather plain compared to the surroundings in which I found myself next. These people seemed quite adept at wood carving, or knew someone who was. Every cupboard, table and piece of furniture carried the same style of ornate carvings I had seen on the outside of the structure.

Noticing my interest, Vocata explained, "The carvings, colors, and various patterns are family designs. Those you see around you are replicated on the hems of our garments. See?" He held up the hem of his skirt for me to examine. I noticed that it was similar to Tabob's, with some slight variations.

"This seems like a lot of work," I interrupted as my eyes traced out the intricate designs stitched into the fabric. "What's the point?"

Smiling condescendingly, Vocata continued, "The purpose is to give us a feeling of unity with our family. Our shared patterns create in us a sense of belonging, so we will always know whom we are a part of. Even a person who makes poor choices knows they can again be accepted by another who wears the same color."

"Why don't you just have the same last name?" I asked.

Vocata stopped walking and gave me a puzzled look.

I shrugged, and explained. "Most people I know have the same last name as one of their parents. A friend of mine, David, is even named after his father."

"Our names serve a different purpose than the patterns, Jeff," retorted Vocata. "Rather than contributing to the feeling of unity that the patterns seek to invoke, our first names identify us as individuals. Our second names identify our occupation or position in society. The second name can change as an individual grows. Tabob, explain to Jeff about your name."

"Well," Tabob hesitantly began. "My second name used to be Ancient, but now is Guard," he said, then fell silent. I waited a moment, but nothing more came. He was no more a man of words at home than he had been in the tunnels.

"He shares that same second name with an older brother, and a host of other fellows from different families," continued Vocata. "His second name was Ancient, after my position. But when he reached manhood, and was chosen as a West Reach Guard, he was given the second name of Guard."

Just then a pretty girl, maybe eight or nine, came running in.

"Tabob!" she screamed as she jumped at the teenage giant. I could tell by his sudden change of expression that he was pleased to see her. Smiling, he returned the girl's bear hug as he caught her, doll-like, in his massive arms. "I have missed you!" she blurted, " Are you back to stay? Can you teach me some more sword-moves? Are you..."

She broke off her barrage of questions as she turned her head and noticed me. Strangely enough, her reaction was not one of scorn or laughing as most of the Inlanders I had met so far. Rather, she just stared at me for a long time. Eventually she smiled, and her face slowly turned red, even to her earlobes.

"This is Jeff," said Vocata, breaking the uncomfortable silence. "He is going to stay with us for a while. Jeff, this is my youngest child, Mib."

"Hi Mib," I said, trying to be polite. Then, seeking to flaunt my new found knowledge, I continued, "We were just talking about second names. Vocata and Tabob have just told me theirs. My second name is Ransford. What's yours?"

Tabob and Mib looked at each other momentarily, then both began to laugh. They continued to giggle even after Vocata tried to silence them with a stern glare.

"I believe what my children are trying to tell you is that females are not usually given a second name in our society until after they marry," explained Vocata as he continued to steel his son and daughter with an icy stare.

Guess I'd better follow Vocata's advice to Tabob to stay alert and learn, I thought, still a little embarrassed by my attempt to show off.

Vocata led the way further into the recesses of his home, and down to a lower level called the eatery. There he introduced me to his wife... and supper.

Miyab (who did have a second name, the same as Vocata's) was a soft spoken but firm individual. Yet she was also very motherly. Anything I asked for or hinted at was served me. Tabob attempted to make jest of my mistake in asking Mib's second name. Miyab ended the discussion with a word and a look that was even more effective than Vocata's attempt. Vocata simply grinned and chuckled to himself.

Miyab was also a good cook. Make that a *great* cook. I feasted on food I had never before seen, but of such flavor and aroma that I easily ate more than what I needed to satiate my ravenous appetite. Miyab reminisced about living at the palace in Coreterior when she was a little girl. She said she had come from a family that had been chefs to Innerland's royalty for generations. What a treat to eat her food after living on my dad's cooking for the past six years! My fast during the long journey to this home had helped to improve my appetite as well.

After eating I felt quite satisfied. We talked some more. The chair I was seated in was plush and comfortable. It was covered in the skin of some velvety animal, as were the others around the room. I didn't recall ever having seen green furry animals before, so I assumed the chair covering had been dyed. As it grew darker, and later, Mib stoked the fire. A cool breeze had come up outside, blowing a flowery smell into the room. The new fire was quite warm, and it caused me to feel even more comfortable and relaxed. Not long after this my thoughts began to turn cloudy, and my world once more turned ebony as I gradually fell into a deep and restful sleep.

-CHAPTER FIVE-
Home Away From Home

I awoke beneath a downy quilt; the air wafting into the room was fresh and bracing. First light was just coming in the three windows on the side of the room. I snuggled further down into the bed awhile even though I was no longer really tired. The mattress was soft; I sunk into its deep folds. The pillow was exceedingly fluffy and formed to my head.

I was disoriented at first. I felt like I had felt when I've stayed in a hotel or spent the night at a friend's house: Odd because I wasn't in the familiar surroundings of my own room, the one I'd woken up in hundreds of times. It was like that now, only I knew where I was. Curiously enough, even though I felt a little disoriented, I now believed that I was here in a place called Innerland, wherever *here* was. But I was also somehow glad of it.

Vocata hinted last night during our first meeting, and then again after supper (or last eats, as they referred to it) that I might be something special. I really didn't know what he was talking about, but it felt good to be wanted. Yes. That was what it was, a feeling of belonging, like I used to feel when I was little, before Mom died. Kind of like what Vocata was talking about with the family patterns all over the house. Family. Wanted. Whatever had brought me here (and at this point I didn't care what it was) I was glad for it and wanted to stay. The softness of the bed only served to add to my overall feeling of well-being.

I dozed off again, reveling in these feelings of contentment. I was interrupted in my slumber by a soft yet persistent knocking. It must have been a long time after I had first stirred because there was a brighter light coming through the side windows of the room. I was still feeling pretty comfortable in bed, so I rolled over and pulled the pillow over my head to try and grab some more shut-eye.

The knocking persisted.

"Yannghhh?" I said towards the door. I had wanted to say something like, "Yes? What do you want?" but that was all that came out.

"Sorry to disturb you, Jeff, but it's late in the morning. Miyab asked me to see if you wanted to break your fast before noonses. Can I tell her you'll be down soon?"

It was Mib.

I sat up in bed, only to realize that I was dressed just in my briefs!

"Uh, just a minute!" I hastily replied. I didn't want anyone coming in to see me dressed like this, or rather, undressed like this.

Looking around I couldn't seem to see where my clothing had been placed. The comfort level I had reveled in all morning was quickly diminishing. I could hear Mib giggling on the other side the door.

"Your clothes are in the keep chest," suggested Mib.

The what? I thought.

As if hearing my question, Mib replied, "It's the large box at the foot of your bed."

Great, I thought, *a family of mind readers. Can you read my mind Mib?* I thought intensely.

Silence.

I stumbled out of bed, dragging half of the coverings with me in an attempt to save my pride should Mib decide to come in while I was dressing. I found my clothes all right, neatly folded in the chest Mib had described. It's funny about trying to do anything in a hurry. It seems to take twice as long to do it because of the nervous fumbles brought about by rushing than if you just settled down and did it calmly. But trying to get dressed with a giggling young girl waiting outside of my door, that for all I knew might come in before I finished, I was anything but calm. In my rush to get my pants on, I tangled my legs and fell forward onto my face in a sore writhing mass, still without my pants quite all the way on. *Ow!*

"Don't worry, Jeff." Mib again. "I won't come in while you're getting dressed." More giggling. This girl must read minds.

When I finally got dressed, flustered, I went and opened the door. Mib stood there with a big grin on her face.

"Mib. Can you read my mind like your father can?" I hissed at her.

"No," she calmly replied with a grin, "I just have two older brothers."

"Oh," was the most intelligent retort I could manage. She motioned for me to follow her down to the eating room, so I did. I had slept on the third level of the house; I still couldn't get over how beautiful all the carvings were. Like I had mentioned, they were all over the place, yet it wasn't gaudy, it just sort of flowed together and looked right. I guess it's kind of like a tree or a forest- there are tons of leaves but they are all in the right place and sort of compliment each other in a way that you don't mind them being all over.

I asked Mib about the carvings and patterns. "Did these take long to do?" I asked, gesturing to the patterns on the bannister bordering the stairs we were walking down.

"All our lives, and those of our mothers and fathers for the last several generations," she replied. Just from the snatches of conversation I had with her, Mib seemed better spoken than most eight year-olds I had previously met. Her comment made me look at the patterns with new respect.

As we continued walking, she asked me a question. "What do you call that clothing you wear on your legs?"

"Pants," I replied.

"Pants," she repeated. "Are they uncomfortable compared to a skirt?"

This time I smiled. "I wouldn't know. Where I come from only girls wear skirts." I said. "And then only sometimes," I added when I thought about most of the girls I saw at school.

"Could you show me how to make... pants?" she asked.

"I would, Mib, but I don't know how. I bought this pair, I didn't make them," I answered, I could tell to her disappointment.

But she persisted. "Could my mother borrow them to copy the pattern?"

"Sure Mib," I replied. I didn't see any harm in this.

When we came to the eating room, on the lowest level, Miyab and Vocata (who had been seated) rose to greet us.

"Good morning, Jeffre..er..Jeff," Miyab corrected herself at a look from Vocata. "I trust you slept well?"

"Very well, thank you. I think I don't remember ever having slept that well before in my life," I replied. She seemed very pleased.

I was still a little nervous about waking up undressed, but I wanted to handle my investigation in a tactful way. "My clothes were nicely folded and put away too. Do I thank you for that?" I asked Miyab.

"Oh no," blushed Miyab, "Vocata insisted that Tabob carry you up to bed after you fell asleep last night."

"Folded clothes and everything. Hmmm. Tabob is coming along," teased Vocata.

As I took my seat I mouthed a silent, "Thank you," to Vocata.

He acknowledged my thanks with a smile and a nod.

Piled in front of us was a thing that looked and smelled like a pancake, only thinner. I watched what the others were doing, and followed suite. They spread a kind of fruit preserve on the thin cakes, then rolled them and ate them. They were quite tasty.

As we were eating, I asked Vocata some questions that had occurred to me. "Innerland is underground, right?"

Vocata nodded. "All of the known Reaches, yes."

"So, how does it get to be day and night?" I asked.

"Is your worl... city so different from ours, Jeff?" queried Vocata, glancing at Mib as he corrected himself.

Miyab and Mib stopped eating and looked at me.

"Well, we have day and night too," I explained. "But we have a star that heats our... city," I said, catching on to Vocata's rue. "It gives us light as well."

Blank stares.

I picked up a roll from a basket on the table to illustrate. "We live on a large ball," I said motioning to the roll in my hand. "It goes around the sun, which is a star. We are always turning, sometimes facing it. Then it is light. And sometimes we face away from it. We are in shadow, and then it is night."

"Imagine, being on the outside of an object," managed Vocata. "Outside is something that exists for us only in legend. Tell me," he continued, "How do you keep from falling off?"

"Oh, that's easy: Gravity," I told him.

"What is... gravity?" asked Vocata.

"Oh, well that's... well... I don't know," I confessed. It was one of those times when I'd wished I had paid a little closer attention in school, so I would know how to explain it.

"What is a stare?" asked Mib, looking at me like she thought I was crazy.

"A star," I corrected. "It's a huge ball of gas that's on fire out in space, but it's so big that it gives off heat and light to our pla... uh, city, even though it's millions of miles away."

"That's amazing," Mib replied sarcastically, as she tried to hide a disbelieving smile. Her parents nodded agreement, Miyab smiling too, but Vocata genuinely looking amazed.

Everyone turned back to the meal.

I continued eating too, and then stopped.

"What about my question?" I asked.

"Oh, sorry, Jeff," replied Vocata as he swallowed a bite of food. "That is due to the ancient race of slowlis that used to inhabit these pockets and caverns."

"Huh?" I managed.

"The slowlis are intelligent animals that eat rock for nourishment." Mib's turn to educate me; She continued, "The babies might be the size of an Inlander. Adults can be up to the size of our house, maybe bigger."

"No one knows for certain, Jeff," interjected Vocata, "Not many people have actually seen a slowlis up close. They have a reputation for being hostile to Inlanders. Some even say that a slowlis would just as soon eat an Inlander as eat a rock! Anyway, the slowlis are the creatures that anciently ate the pockets and caverns out from the rock, the same caverns in which we now make our cities. After eating the rock, they secreted a substance that glows for about ten to twelve hours, and then goes dark for a proportional time, giving us our day and night cycle."

"That's amazing," I replied. It seemed as appropriate a response as any.

"The last deliverer led us to these caverns when the place we inhabited began to wear out and become cold and dark," said Vocata. He emphasized the word last, and gave me a knowing look. I wasn't sure why. "That was about three hundred cycles ago," he added, "Where it was we migrated from is not known. There weren't very good records kept that many cycles ago."

We continued eating for a while longer, just making small talk. Then all of a sudden Mib made an announcement. "Miyab? Jeff said you could borrow his pants today when we went out so that you could fashion some for me."

I nearly choked on my breakfast, as I thought about walking around a town filled with people, and me pant-less!

"That's nice, Mib," Miyab acknowledged, "I could start on them this afternoon if you'd like. Are you all right, Jeff?" she asked, as she noticed me choking.

Probably knowing what I was thinking, Vocata again came to my rescue. "Miyab made some clothing for you that would be, well, let's say a little less conspicuous. We thought it would be good if you accompanied Mib today, dressed as an Inlander from West Reach. No one besides this family would know otherwise. Mib could show you around our homelands and the surrounding areas before she takes noonses to Tabob. You and I could talk some more later this afternoon." Then he added in a whisper, as he pulled me aside, "It would be good for now if you kept your identity a secret. I will explain why later."

I didn't like the idea of wearing a dress. But then I thought of how these people had shown such kindness to me and how they had accepted me. Still torn between conflicting feelings, I hesitated.

Miyab looked at me. "I made the kilt in our family colors," she stated, then added hopefully, "If that's acceptable."

That clinched it. "I would be honored to wear your family colors," I decided. Smiling, and setting down my half eaten rolled cake, I said, "Let me at that kilt!" I guess I said the right thing because Miyab beamed.

After trying on the kilt, I looked at my image in the mirror and reflected on my judgment of Tabob the morning before. I suppose I'd always believed that what goes around comes around, but I didn't think that included me having to wear a dress! I felt like a dork wearing a tee shirt and basketball shoes with un-matching skirt. *Oh well*, I thought, *It doesn't look too bad. Miyab is a good seamstress because it fits well. Besides,* I continued to justify to myself, *Everyone else is dressed this way too.*

As I came out of the room in which I changed, Miyab clucked her approval as she rotated around me. Mib just stared at me smiling and blushing like at our first meeting yesterday.

"OK?" I asked Vocata.

"OK." he confirmed, nodding his head affirmatively. "You will pass though West Reach and the countryside as if you were Mib's companion and a fellow Inlander to all eyes that see you."

I thanked Miyab for the clothes and for a good breakfast, and then we departed. I felt more comfortable walking along the street with

Mib as I realized that all of the other people had on clothing similar to mine, and that they weren't staring at me so noticeably today. The only variations were the colors and patterns on the hems, some of which were more complicated, some less so. As we walked and visited back and forth I was encouraged by one other thing- I was glad they had let me keep my Captain Amazing tee shirt!

-CHAPTER SIX-
Mib, and Gum-Paste

Mib and I became fast friends. She said she was about eight, almost nine cycles old. I didn't at first know what a cycle was, but I think it roughly equated to one of our years, so she would end up being about four or five years younger than me. I had never really hung around any third or fourth graders since I'd been one. Come to think of it, I never really hung around anybody much in middle school either, except maybe superficially. After awhile it did not seem too odd. I suppose some people just naturally hit it off together- that's the way it was with Mib and me. I felt comfortable around her, and she seemed to feel at ease around me.

At first we just walked and talked. It was nice to be dressed as an Inlander and not receive the strange looks and laughs that had been given me the day before. No one thought my tee shirt and basketball shoes too odd, I guess because the rest of my dress made me fit in.

It was difficult to fathom just how many people lived in West Reach; there must have been several thousand. Mib said that her family had made their home here for generations, and added that it was somewhat small compared to many of the other towns, especially when you got closer to Coreterior: the ruling town where the Great Center Judge had his palace.

Mib was pretty good about answering my questions too, of which I had many. For example, I asked her about the glowing stick Tabob had used yesterday afternoon to light our way through the darkened tunnels. She claimed it was not made of wood at all, but was a bone from one of the slowlis creatures Vocata had mentioned earlier that morning.

"How do you make it glow on the end," I asked curiously.

"We don't. It does that by itself," she replied flatly. "The slowlis glows, or so I'm taught. I've never seen a live one. Tabob took me on an exploration once to find a slowlis skeleton. The bones are worth a great deal in barter."

"What was it like?" I asked.

"Well," Mib continued, "At first I was scared because it was so big! Tabob reassured me that it had long been dead, and so I was alright after that. It was beautiful, and such a bright light surrounded it that I had to squint my eyes in order to see clearly."

"Why are the bones so valuable?"

"I think because they always glow. They do not seem to follow a day-night cycle like the smearing on the walls," replied Mib.

"That's interesting stuff by the way," I mentioned, "I got some on my hand yesterday when I smeared my hand against one of the cave walls."

Mib stopped and looked at me questioningly. "You should not have been able to do that unless the tunnel was very fresh, like a day old. Maybe two days at the very most!" she exclaimed. "You should not go back to those tunnels. You risk meeting a slowlis if you do, and many of my friends say that a slowlis would sooner eat an Inlander than rock!"

"I'll keep that in mind," I said as I thought about the fact that the tunnel she was referring to seemed to be connected to a hole in my bedroom wall. Upon thinking this, I remembered the image of my father towering kilometers above me as I began my explorations of the tunnels that led to West Reach. Could that have been real too, or was that part actually my imagination? I hadn't pieced all of this together, yet if this was some tiny civilization, it fit in somehow with something my mom taught me once. I was fairly little at the time, and was killing some bugs (ants, maybe earwigs or something.) Anyway, there I was having this great fun and not really thinking I was doing any harm. Mom saw me, grabbed me up in her arms (quite upset and crying) and made me promise to never maliciously kill again… especially tiny creatures. I remember her sharing with me just before she died, her belief that there were worlds within worlds, all interconnected somehow. It seemed kind of weird at the time, and I didn't pay much attention to it, happier simply to be with Mom than really concerned with what she was saying. Trying to figure out my location now, those memories tugged at my mind.

Mib and I continued to traipse about the outreaches (what she called the outskirts of her city) for a few more hours. I had noticed a few shrubs and trees when I arrived yesterday. Today I was fascinated by the great variety of trees and plant life, and how wide this land all felt. It was only when I looked straight up, through the dense roof of trees that I remembered that this entire city, the countryside, and the whole of Innerland, according to Mib, were contained within giant connected caverns.

Some of the trees were similar to those I had seen in my world: brown or grey trunks with a variety of green foliage, and of different heights.

Strange, I thought, *how I seem to be more readily accepting that this is another world. It doesn't even bother me to do so anymore, and this is only my second day here.*

Back to the flora: Most of the trees in the forest were like a combination between an evergreen and a leafy tree; both needles and leaves grew from the same cluster. Mib identified this more common tree as the musk tree, because of the perfumed smell of the wood when cut. It also bore a sweet tasting edible nut. Because of the vast forested regions of musk, it was the material most of their buildings were constructed of.

More obvious differences were evident with the animals, of which there was quite a variety. My favorite was called a glib. It acted like a squirrel, in that it ran up and down trees. But it looked more like something out of a bedtime story. It was kind of green (like many things I had seen here) covered with baggy looking leathery skin, and about as long (from head to tail) as my entire arm. Oh, and it was fast, very fast. We would usually see about ten glibs playing about on the ground. When they noticed our approach they would scatter to the protective canopy of the surrounding musk trees before we got within three meters. From the treetops they were safe to hurtle nutshells and insults at us.

The glibs made a call that sounded like, "Chiip chiip cheee cheee cheee cheeeeee." Though a small animal, their calls echoed and reverberated through the vast forests. Mib said these were fairly intelligent animals, and that people had been known to tame them as pets.

"My father used to tell me stories about a pet glib he had named Chimmery," Mib shared. "They used to get into all kind of mischief when he was a boy."

Her tale interested me, so we tried to coax some glibs to come get food from us. I didn't make a pet that day, but I was able to eventually lure one feisty young glib into taking a crust of roll from my hand! I felt pretty good about that accomplishment. It was more than I had ever gotten the squirrels to do back home.

The hue of the cattle, horses and other farm animals (the breed and use of which I didn't know) was green too. When I mentioned how funny I thought this was to Mib, she gave me a quizzical look, then commented rather sarcastically, "What color are they where you come from, brown, because of the stare you told us about at breakfast?" I just smiled and remained quiet. I began to realize that just because I expected things to be similar to what I'd seen, it didn't mean everything in existence had to fit my current worldview. This realization made it easier for me to begin to accept the reality of Innerland.

About lunchtime (I could tell the time by the hunger pangs in my stomach) we came across the construction site where Tabob was working.

"I thought he was a guard," I mentioned to Mib.

"He is," she replied matter-of-factly, "But he also helps to construct new buildings in his off-time. Since we are never really at war with any of the other settlements these days, it is more of a ceremonial job than a full time occupation."

I didn't at first identify the partially completed building that we were approaching as a construction site, mainly because there was no telltale pounding of hammers and machinery that I had become accustomed to hearing when around such a site before.

When we reached the building under construction, I noticed some saws being used. Each consisted of a bow with a blade stretched taught between the two ends. I immediately identified the musk tree smell: it was heavy sweet, yet not overpowering. The thing that fascinated me was how the workers got the timbers in the building to stay attached to one another without nails or spikes. Those attaching the boards would brush a gooey substance on one surface, and then carefully place the second plank firmly against the first. The peculiar thing was that it held. Tightly. I was curious about this sticky phenomenon, as I had been with most things I had seen since my recent arrival. As we sat down to eat our noonses together, I asked Tabob about his super-glue.

"What is that stuff you are using to hold the building together, Tabob?"

"Gum paste? Oh, it's a substance we get from a certain type of tree in the Highland Forest," replied Tabob between chews.

Mib explained further, "The people who live in Highland cut the trees and bleed the paste a little at a time into buckets. We trade them for glow sticks we craft from the slowlis skeletons we find that I told you about earlier."

Tabob stopped eating and stared at his sister.

"Don't worry," defended Mib, "I didn't tell Jeff where the dying place was where we get the bones."

Tabob seemed satisfied by this answer, and turned back to his meal.

"Not that Jeff would tell if he knew," she defended as she turned back to look at me.

"Harumph," stated Tabob with a mouthful of food. Clearly he was annoyed with his sister for even mentioning it to me. It must have been a really important find.

After we had finished eating, Tabob and the others went back to working. I asked him if I could watch for a few minutes before Mib and I headed back.

"Sure, Jeff," he invited with a cheesy smile. Tabob carefully painted some gum paste at the level he had left off on, and then turned to get a board.

Just how sticky was this stuff? Being ever curious, I leaned forward and placed the tip of my pointer finger firmly in the goo that had just been painted on.

"Jeff, no!" screamed Mib, just a fraction of a second too late.

Tabob began to laugh wholeheartedly. He was soon joined by some of the other youth who were working nearby. Wondering what the big deal was I pulled my finger back towards myself. Only when I pulled, it didn't come back. *Great*, I thought, *now I know why Tabob was so eager to let me watch.*

Soon the workers tired of the game, and went back to what they were doing. By the time they tired of laughing, I not only felt embarrassed, but my face was crimson with anger.

"I'll get you unstuck, if you promise to make me a shirt like yours," offered Tabob, knowing he had me in an awkward situation. "There is no known solvent," he added, trying to convince me, "And only I know how to get you unstuck."

I finally said I would agree to the deal, feeling glad that at least I hadn't been stupid enough to put my whole hand in the goo when I tested it.

"One more thing," he said with a smirk of deviltry.

"Name it," I said resignedly.

"Make it a drawing of me," he demanded.

"I'll see what I can do."

With the agreement sealed, Tabob carefully wrapped his enormous right hand around my pointer finger, and yanked!

"Ahhhhhh!" I screamed. It felt like the end of my finger was gone. Looking back at the wall I had just touched, I realized that it was! Well, at least the skin that had covered my fingertip; it was still stuck to the place it had been just a few moments before while still attached to me.

Tabob still held my finger, which by this time was bleeding freely. Tearing a makeshift bandage from a rag laying on a bench beside him, he deftly wrapped the end of my finger to staunch the flow of blood.

I felt conflicting emotions about this situation. Tabob had allowed me to do a stupid thing with no prior warning, which made me mad. But on the other hand, he was saving me from my own stupid mistake, for which he had my gratitude. Because he was my new friend's brother, not because I particularly liked him, I opted to be gracious about the situation and thanked him for his assistance.

"Don't worry, Jeff," he admonished between chuckles while he wrapped my finger. "Almost everyone touches the Gum Paste. Once. Why even Mib..."

Before he could continue, a red-faced Mib snatched my hand from his, and cut him off. She did not take the same approach towards her brother that I had chosen.

"Be quiet!" She screamed at Tabob in a commanding tone. "Jeff is here as our guest, not as an enemy to be taken advantage of. Come on, Jeff," she encouraged as she took my hand and began walking away from the construction site. Tabob just stood there with his mouth open. I don't think Mib had ever yelled at him before, judging by his stupefied reaction.

Later, Mib showed me the scars on the palms of her hands, and knees where she had tried to crawl across a surface painted with the paste when she was three.

"How did they get you off?" I asked.

"Tabob's method is the only way known," she replied with a shudder, probably remembering how it must have hurt.

I replied with a sympathetic grimace.

"Like he said, almost everyone tries it… once," she said with a smirk. "I haven't gone too close to gum paste since then."

"I think I'll be swearing off the stuff myself," I said returning her smile. She's a cute girl, I thought as we continued to walk together. She would sure be a neat little sister.

"I'm sorry that I acted that way," Mib apologized, after we had walked for a few minutes more. "I just didn't like him treating you like that."

"It was OK," I said. "I appreciate you coming to my rescue, buddy."

"Buddy?"

"It's a word that means you're my friend," I explained.

"Oh. You're welcome… buddy," she whispered. Suddenly blushing and giggling, she skipped down the worn path ahead of me a few paces.

-CHAPTER SEVEN-
The Great Center Judge, Gamious

It became my routine for the next several days to accompany Mib as she took noonses to Tabob at his work-site. I think the reason Vocata asked me to be Mib's daily companion on her wanderings was as much for my benefit as it was for hers: she was familiar with the goings on of the village enough to take care of herself, even though my coming here had Vocata worried for some reason. Through my wanderings I became more familiar with the workings of this place than I would have sitting at Vocata's home all day visiting; although, I truly enjoyed my conversations with that affectionate old man each afternoon.

I think after the third afternoon visit, Vocata finally believed me when I told him for probably the fifteenth time that I really didn't know why I was here, but that I wanted to stay. I told him that I was beginning to feel like part of his family. He and his wife Miyab both were extremely pleased by this statement. I felt I was becoming close to this little group in less than a week. Closer than I felt to the family that was really my own; except when my mom was alive, of course. Her being a part of the family was so long ago though, that I could remember it only by feelings. And that was the way this group felt. Family.

Even with the closeness, there were a lot of unknowns. Like, where was I really? I had given up the notion that I was dreaming that first evening. I recalled the vice-like grip Vocata had crushed my hand in. Dreams don't feel that real. Nor had I ever noticed the intimate details of life in a dream. Come to think of it, I had never noticed this many details in my own world either. I couldn't fully explain it, but Innerland was a real place. I just didn't know *where* it was.

I remember walking down the tunnels. I had started out walking down a pinhole tunnel. This must be the world of itty, bitty, tiny, small, people that live inside of a pinhole in the wall of my family home! *Right*. That idea seemed as likely to me as the idea that I was still dreaming. *A microscopic world?* Give me a break! Whatever this was, it wasn't science fiction. My dad's family had lived in our old home for generations though. Perhaps the ancient building was some kind of portal to another reality. But why hadn't anyone else ever found it out? And more pertinent, *how* had I found it? When I got to wondering, it occurred to me that it didn't really matter; I was here. I was happy. Happier than I had been since my mother had died. The reality of this situation mattered more to me than all of the wondering and answers in the world. Right now I had my answer. It entailed being part of a family, even if not my own, that loved me. Well, everyone except maybe Tabob, and the brother I hadn't yet met.

Tabob did like the picture I was drawing of him though, no matter what he might have thought of me personally. Miyab had really gotten angry with Tabob for tricking me and said that, "A promise made under distress is not binding." Even though she said I didn't have to make a shirt for Tabob, I followed through on our agreement. I have to admit that the body of pulsating muscles that I drew was based more on Captain Amazing's renditions in comic books than on Tabob's physique. However Tabob remained the only one in the family blissfully unaware of that fact. He commented on how the drawing was an amazing likeness of him, but could I make the shoulders a little broader? After experimenting with some dyes, wax, and loosely woven cloth, I was able to print a fairly nice silk screen for Tabob. He really liked it, and I felt that I grew in his esteem when I presented it to him.

On about the eighth day in West Reach, Mib and I were walking through the forest of musk trees towards Tabob's construction site. It was the last day we were to go that path because they were finishing up the structure that afternoon. The chattering glibs scattered, as usual. We noticed many newborn glibs with their parents. A little ahead of us, on the ground, was a still green form, nestled in a different shade of grass. I approached it to find it was a baby glib. It wasn't moving, and its parent screamed at us from the treetops, just out of our reach. I picked up the glib. It moved slightly, and appeared to be hurt.

"Why doesn't the mother come and take it back up the tree with her?" I asked Mib.

"I don't think she can," replied Mib. "When an animal is hurt, it is usually left by its kind to die. Glibs are fun, Jeff, but have no ability to care for their sick and injured as the Inlanders do. "Besides," she added, "The animal has your scent now, from your touching it. Its parent won't take it back now."

As I held the tiny glib in my hand, I felt guilty about picking it up. From what Mib told me though, it wouldn't have survived anyway. I didn't know what else to do, so I moved to place it back beneath the tree. The parent had stopped screeching by this time, and had joined the other glibs in their foraging further up in the canopy of leaves. As I placed the tiny injured glib on the ground, it looked at me, a wanting in its eyes. The look conveyed more than just desire; there was intelligence in the creature's gaze. An idea suddenly occurred to me as I reflected on what Mib told me when I had first seen a group of glibs. I approached her with a suggestion.

"Mib, remember what you told me about your father several days ago? How he had a pet glib as a boy?"

Grinning, she gave me a knowing look. It was great to have become close enough friends that she seemed to know what I was going to say before I'd phrased it.

"Do you think your father could help us heal this little fellow? Maybe even teach us to train him?" I asked.

Wearing a full-blown smile now, she replied, "If not Father, then no one!"

I wrapped the little animal in the folds of my jacket. If I thought an animal could have the ability to smile, I would have to say that this one was. As the glib looked up at me with an affectionate, contented gaze, I wondered if it had really been my original idea to care for it after all.

Tabob shared his perspective that he thought it was a waste of time to try training a glib. He thought that we should put it out of its misery. However, when he proposed this he quickly backed off when Mib started into him again, even angrier than when Tabob had tricked me into touching the gum paste. After Mib started on him, Tabob quickly finished his noonses and got back to work, before anyone else! Mib and I joked about it on the way home. I was glad that Tabob was, for once, the brunt of our humor.

The glib recovered quickly. Mib and I agreed to share our new pet fifty-fifty, but he had a tendency to like to sleep on my shoulders while we walked. Since he slept a lot, this meant he was with me during most of the time. However, since he was equally amiable towards us both, Mib didn't seem to mind. We named the glib

'Pounce' because of his tendency to jump on our faces unawares and start licking us when we overslept and he was hungry. He would also act characteristic of his name when one of us forgot to feed him and Miyab left an open plate of food out. Pounce! It would disappear. Our twosome soon became a trio as Pounce learned to live in civilization. The plates of food ceased to disappear quite as frequently, much to Miyab's relief. Even Tabob once admitted that Pounce seemed to be a pretty intelligent animal. That was a generous comment, coming from Tabob.

Mib and I aimlessly wandered home one especially warm afternoon after sharing noonses with Tabob and his buddies. It was during the second month (according to my reckoning) of my stay with Vocata's family. Something I had heard Vocata say to Tabob when reprimanding him that first evening crossed my mind. Pounce basked in the afternoon glow from the cavern walls as I contemplated my question. Neither Vocata nor Tabob had said anything about it since, and I had learned that some things in this world were not as openly talked about as others. Even so, Mib had been quite willing to answer my barrage of questions so far, so I approached her with this curiosity too. I decided the best strategy was to be direct.

"Mib, What is Eighth Cycle?"

Turning, she flashed her frequent smile. "That's part of our religion," she stated.

Oh, I thought, Perhaps I shouldn't have asked.

But I guess it was alright, because she then went on to explain, "Every eight cycles we pay homage to the Deliverer by trekking to the Great Door: it has been closed since he last visited here. We bring gifts of things he may need during his sojourn through our world. There are still people alive who have seen him, though they are mostly the ancient ones like my father. He hasn't come for many cycles, some say it's because most people have stopped believing in him these days. But some of us still believe, and so every eighth cycle we go to the Great Door to offer gifts. Too bad you missed the celebration; it finished just a few days before you arrived in town."

I decided not to tell just yet that I had been on the other side of that door... Recently.

"What did this Deliverer deliver you from?" I asked, even more curious now.

"Are you from that far out of town?" Mib asked, her occasional sarcastic tone returning.

"I would sincerely like to know," I stated flatly, stopping now to stare at her more seriously.

"Sorry," she grinned, "I thought you were teasing me. I guess I am too used to Tabob and his friend Jured playing jokes on me. Well, my father told you the first part of the story a while ago."

"Oh?" I remarked, thinking back on my many conversations with Vocata.

"About how the Deliverer came over three hundred cycles ago and led our civilizations from a cold, dark, and dead world to Innerland," she reminded me.

I nodded my head to indicate that I recalled Vocata mentioning that.

We were now just a few blocks from Mib's house. I was glad my sense of direction (or location) seemed to still be functional in that underground country.

"He ruled here for a time," Mib continued, as we took a shortcut through an alleyway, "He was said to be very wise, and just. The Deliverer fell in love with an Inlander, married her, and turned the ruling back over to the people. He eventually took his bride to live with him in his world, though they returned once many cycles later. I have been told that..."

Mib didn't get a chance to finish her sentence, because as we rounded a corner, a carriage drawn by eight green-colored and mean looking horses came careening with reckless abandon down the lane. I turned Mib around quickly and pushed her back into the alley we had just exited, narrowly missing being trampled by the horses myself. Pounce jumped to the safety of an overhanging ledge. In a fit of anger, I grabbed the nearest loose stone and hurled it with great force at the rear of the quickly receding carriage. Not ever having been one for sports, I was surprised at the velocity and accuracy of my throw; it sounded as though the rock broke wood!

I didn't have time to admire my lucky shot though, because no sooner did it leave my hand than I heard the thundering of many horsemen behind me, then just as suddenly I was flattened by a heavy airborne body that knocked the wind out of me. Struggling to regain my breath and turn over on my back, I got my first glimpse of the attacker, who was already standing and had unsheathed a spear.

"In the name of the Almighty Great Center Judge! Who dares to attack his royal person?" boomed the voice of this muscular looking soldier. I thought he was being a little melodramatic.

Lying on the ground in the dust, still trying to get a deep breath, but madder than Hades, I replied while gesturing down the road at the direction the coach had careened. "The driver of that coach is mad! He almost hit my friend and me; he's the one you should be jumping on!" I thought I was being quite bold; especially when I realized that this clown was only one of about ten equally mean looking chaps.

"Well boy," he spat, "It was an honest mistake. But since that was the carriage of the Great Center Judge Gamious, it is the last mistake you will ever make!"

I felt inclined to agree with him, as his spear came whistling towards my unprotected chest.

-CHAPTER EIGHT-
Sentence of Execution

It's amazing how in certain situations you seem to notice more detail about things around you. This was one of those times for me.

As the soldier's spear accelerated swiftly towards my chest (intent on piercing my heart) for some odd reason I noticed incredible detail about him and his weapon. For example, I noted that the fellow looked remarkably like Tabob, yet with a mean scowl that slurred his otherwise handsome features. His green toned leather kilt did not boast the designs I had seen on other Inlanders, but instead had stitches of gold thread running along the lower fringe. He also wore a black leather breastplate, complete with triangular guard pieces fixed over his shoulders. In the center of the breastplate (which caught and held my gaze) he wore a circular golden talisman bordered by the same gold thread as was on his kilt's hem.

The auburn sphere glowed subtly, beautifully, and I could only gawk at it as the spear continued to rush towards my heart. I didn't move. I knew I should, it was just that the infernal glowing kept my eyes fixed. I couldn't move. I was about to die, to be skewered in a world I didn't fully understand and which was not my own. The double edged, tear-drop shaped spear with gold accents was now a single centimeter away from my chest, ready to puncture my flesh...

"HOLD!"

The harshly familiar voice of command broke the hypnotic spell of the sphere. I came to myself in time to see the spear that would have taken my life harmlessly deflected hilt deep into the wood of the building on my left. I instinctively rolled to a defensive stance to the right, and attempted to gain my footing. My head was a little fuzzy. I felt as though I had just awakened from a strange dream.

Vocata stood over me, wrapped in a brown cloak. He held a staff of glowing ivory horizontally between himself and my would-be-murderer while I raised myself to one knee. Neither Vocata nor my attacker moved for what seemed a very long time. Meanwhile, the coach that had almost hit us had turned and was heading back to our position, at a leisurely pace.

"Father," mumbled the spearman, his hard features softening in the sudden confusion he apparently felt.

"Corun," hissed Vocata not bothering to hide the contempt in his voice. "So, oldest son, is this what you forsook the family colors for, to become a cold-blooded-murderer of defenseless children? What an *honorable* choice," scolded Vocata emphasizing his sarcasm. "Did you not remember anything I taught you as a child at my knee?"

By this time Mib had come out of the alley and was helping me to my feet, brushing the dust from my back and arms. Vocata remained between the two of us and Corun. So, Corun was his son. No wonder he looked like Tabob. I had begun to think I was stereotyping the bodybuilders I kept crossing paths with when I first thought the brothers looked alike. I noticed that Mib would not look directly at Corun, and she clenched her teeth tightly. I was relieved to see that she was alright, and that Pounce had climbed to her shoulder. The coach had returned by the time I was standing, and the door was just opening when Corun tried to make a defense.

"Father, I... he..."

"What goes on here, Corun, Second Head Guard?" questioned a handsome figure that had just emerged from the interior of the coach. The new fellow was decked out in lush, rich looking robes of many hued green. He wore a golden coronet upon his head, and a golden disk on his breastplate, similar to the one Corun wore which had had such a hypnotic effect on me. He also wore a short pointed beard and moustache- the first Inlander I had seen, I realized, that wore any facial hair. Fifteen to twenty other soldiers had come with the return of the coach. If ever I regretted a rash act, I, at this time, regretted the anger that caused me to throw that stupid rock!

"Guard!" he shouted. "Is your loyalty to me, or to someone else?" Beard-Face asked as his mouth formed into a sly grin. His gaze shifted towards Vocata. In the same way that I had impressions that led me to trust Vocata upon our first meeting, I had feelings that also led me to form an opinion about this new arrival. I didn't like him. I did not feel I could trust him, nor did I want to listen to him. I had a very uneasy feeling even being in his presence.

"Forgive me, Gamious, oh Great One," groveled Corun, "But this boy threw a rock at your carriage as you traveled by. I was stopping to question him," he lied. So, Beard-Face was the Great Judge Gamious. I had really picked the wrong target! "This man," he continued, gesturing towards his father, "Interrupted me in my duties."

This man? I thought, *You jerk! You were just calling him Father a moment ago.*

"I see you have relearned other things as well, son," murmured Vocata under his breath.

Gamious smiled wickedly, then walked to the back of the carriage, and attempted (unsuccessfully) to dislodge the rock that I had thrown from the wooden frame of the carriage. The rock was imbedded deeply. Frowning, and giving up in the attempt to dislodge the stone, he turned and walked over to me.

"Was that meant for me?" Beard-Face demanded in a hysterically raised voice as he pointed to the half visible rock.

"Sir, I was angry. I did not mean to hurt anyone. I only wanted to let off some steam from my anger," I recanted, trying to use a little more wisdom than when I chucked the rock at his coach.

"Whence came your anger towards me?" Gamious asked, in a falsely concerned, almost hypnotic voice.

"The coach you were in almost ran over my companion and me," I replied, meeting his gaze squarely.

Gamious returned my gaze momentarily, and then turned back to Corun.

"What is the law, Second Head Guard?"

"Death to any who dares make an attempt on the life of the Great Center Judge," he replied, like he was repeating a rotely memorized line.

"But I didn't- "I was stopped mid-sentence in my defense as two burly guards, who had worked their way around behind me, forced me to my knees. Pain jolted up my legs and lower back. All I could do was gasp in an attempt to finish what I had begun to say.

Vocata stepped regally forward. "That is not the law of the Deliverer," he defied, staring unafraid into the visage of Gamious.

Gamious returned Vocata's gaze for a moment, then turned and began ranting, "Are you the Deliverer, Vocata?" he asked mockingly. "How about your daughter, eh?" Mib hid her face in the cowls of her father's cape. "Perhaps this old man," Gamious said as he gestured to a fellow who had become part of the rapidly growing crowd. "Perhaps," he paused, and then gestured towards me, "Perhaps this little boy, who threw the rock, is your Deliverer." I had about had it with the little boy hang-up everyone seemed to have about me.

Gamious turned away from me, began to walk around the inside circle of the small crowd, raised his hands, and began a seemingly well-rehearsed speech. "The Deliverer, if ever there truly was one, is not here. I, Gamious Judge, am ruler. My word is law. I have brought peace and prosperity, and the promise of more than this people have ever imagined."

"The Deliverer will return, *noble* Gamious," countered Vocata. "I am beginning to see that there may be more of a need than I had previously supposed."

"Who will stand with Vocata in perpetuating this superstitious belief of a Deliverer?" challenged Gamious. "Let them speak now, or remain silent!"

Other than Mib, who stood proudly next to her father, no one came forward. Many people cast their eyes down, as if ashamed. Then, from the ranks of the soldiers, came a yell, "Hail, most noble Gamious!"

The other soldiers picked up and echoed the cry. A few people in the gathering crowd halfheartedly began to join in, but were quickly suppressed by the stern looks of their peers. As I was being hustled off to the carriage, my eyes picked Vocata out of the crowd for an instant. I held my ground, and as our gaze met, I heard in my mind, *We will not leave you to die, Jeff!*

I probably would have enjoyed my ride to the palace more if I had not been tied to the top of the carriage! Between the occasional clouds of dust and the tightness of my bonds, I was more than a little uncomfortable. I had no more intention of throwing rocks, so the ropes probably didn't need to be quite so tight. Corun had taken the honor of tying me up, and attacked the task with great relish. He must not have paid very close attention to his father when he taught him how to tie knots though, because with a little pulling and prying on my part, the ropes stretched out enough to at least be bearable.

I rode, trussed up like a calf in a rodeo, for about an hour. Mib was right: as we neared what I supposed must be Coreterior, the towns became more frequent, and more populated. As the population grew denser, the forests and greenery fell away to numerous buildings. I saw very little of these because of the swiftness of our passage. One image that stayed in my mind though, was that of a little girl sitting in the dust by the edge of the road. I wasn't sure at the time why that particular memory remained with me, but I can still see her lithe little form, her downcast eyes. I wondered why she looked frail, so sad.

The air became thicker with dust as we neared the palace, until I thought I would choke on the constant swirling particles of dirt. The palace itself was amazing. Catching glimpses of it (as my head lolled from side to side atop the carriage) I got the impression of a medieval castle... and its reflection! How much more beautiful than the squalor on the border of the city. Gamious fared far better than the people under his direct rule. The towers reached from the cavern floor to the ceiling, almost a kilometer above. There were six towers on the outer wall, and one immense tower in the center of the courtyard that was larger around than the rest.

Well, instead of being given the master tour, I got the budget version: across the courtyard to a front guard tower, dragged down what seemed like thousands of steps, to a dank, musty cellar. There may not have been exactly a thousand steps, but the fact that I kept tripping up in the dark as I was hauled downward made it seem like there were.

I was eventually led through several hallways to a cell door. In the middle of the door was a small window-like opening, about a third of a meter square, with four bars running vertically. The door was opened, and I was abruptly hurled into the awaiting darkness. The overwhelming smell that accosted my nostrils was as offensive as the pile of gush that broke my fall. The mound I arose from smelled like something one might step in while in a cow field, yet I knew that the pile had not come from cattle. Needless to say, I removed myself from its immediate location, even if that meant only to the other side of the small room.

So far everything about this encounter stank (no pun intended) except for the detail I noticed when Corun tried to kill me; so indelibly etched into my mind was that conflict that I should be able to produce an accurately detailed rendition of it on paper. Later of course, when I had some paper and light, and was safe. If there would be a later when I was safe. Somehow, even in these disgusting circumstances, I believed in Vocata. Though an old man, he was becoming like a super hero to me. He had already saved my life once, and he would somehow save me again. I just had a feeling.

As the long hours wore on into night, I realized that no one would be bringing me any supper. I was glad I had eaten well two times earlier today, but I still felt like I was starving... starving, and bored. What I wouldn't have given for a sketchpad or a comic book that night. Eventually, even with the caustic odor (that I somehow didn't get used to) I was able to doze into a fitful sleep. There was nothing else to do, and I figured I'd need my strength for whatever lay ahead.

* * *

My 'trial' the next day was a complete sham. I didn't quite feel ready for it, smelling the way I did. And I didn't feel that one partially filled bucket of cold water, dumped over my head, was enough to clean me sufficiently. Gamious must have agreed with me about my smell, because he had me situated a good ten meters from him during the proceedings.

Several witnesses (in addition to Corun, who had tried to kill me) claimed that I had said things like, "Down with the Great Center Judge," and, "Death to Gamious!" The last claim was almost funny, especially upon recalling that I didn't even know the Great Center Judge's name prior to meeting him. I hope you'll believe me by this time when I say that I'm a fairly observant person. Though there was a small crowd there yesterday, I don't remember seeing one of those witnesses (besides Corun himself) actually there at the alley when I threw the rock.

Gamious seemed amused as each new witness added their story. I had an idea that his whole purpose in having this trial was not so much to convict me, but to get one up on Vocata. Gamious continued to smile and eat a leisurely breakfast of multi-colored fruit as the false-witnesses spoke. That fruit sure looked good to me after missing supper last night. Vocata and Mib were there also, but they remained silent throughout the accusations.

When I was finally given a chance to speak, I was feeling more nervous than ever about the possibility that things might not work out how I wanted them to after all. So, trying to be polite, I simply apologized to Gamious, and promised I would never throw a rock at his carriage, ever again. It didn't seem to appease him.

"Grovel now," spat Gamious, "But it is too late for that to make any difference."

Boy! This guy could sure use some of the mercy and wisdom in judgment that Mib said that the Deliverer had.

Vocata finally broke his silence. "You cannot have him killed," he pleaded.

"Why?" asked Gamious sarcastically while plopping another grape into his open mouth.

"Because... He is from Otherworld," stated Vocata evenly.

The assemblage gasped, and Gamious looked as though he were going to choke on his grape. When he recovered, he got an evil glint in his eye, and commanded, "Then show me the Stone of Recognition!"

When Vocata turned his eyes downward, and responded, barely audibly, "He doesn't seem to have it, your Greatness," Gamious just laughed, long and loud. It wasn't the kind of laughter that made you want to join in on the joke either. It was an evil, chilling, horrifying, laugh that made me feel as though I were doomed. I did not feel any hope remaining in the situation.

"Send for the entourage of guards," commanded the judge. "Jef-Re will be taken to the lair of the slowlis to be consumed by the monster." What a jerk! Gamious thought he knew me well enough to pass a death sentence on me, and yet didn't even know I preferred to be called Jeff.

Mib screamed. Pounce began to chatter wildly. Vocata silently stared at Gamious, his eyes filled with seething hatred. Corun looked as though he were fighting a sort of inward battle, which his loyalties to Gamious must have won, because he viciously jerked me to my feet, and began to drag me, half stumbling, toward the holding cells.

I hollered something unkind at Gamious; I think it made him blush. Almost as soon as my words were out of my mouth, I was knocked unconscious by one of my captors. I awoke somewhat later, trussed up as the day before, only this time on a flatbed wagon. My head felt as though it had been broken open in the back, and ached terribly; especially as I rolled from side to side on the hard timbers of the wagon bed.

From what I could discern, there were no longer any villages or townships surrounding me. For as far as I could see, there stretched a forest of musk trees so thick that they nearly choked out the trail. As I fell in and out of wakefulness, I sincerely hoped that this 'slowlis' fellow was not as bad as everybody made him out to be.

-CHAPTER NINE-
Ker-Lee and His Stooges

The wagon ride to my decreed doom was only slightly more comfortable than the ride to the palace atop the Center Judge's carriage had been. My arms were becoming severely sore and chafed, even though I had again been able to work the ropes a little loose. I was not overly impressed with the guards' rope tying abilities. I had dropped out of the Boy Scouts after only a couple of months, yet I could tie a better knot than these guys. However, their lack of ability allowed me to get the ropes loose, which in turn enabled me to be a little more comfortable; I wasn't going to complain to them about it.

The entourage of guards numbered sixteen. I was flattered. They must have really thought me a dangerous criminal. I still regretted having thrown the rock, but there was a new regret added to this: I regretted not having hit Gamious!

After Vocata's revelation that I was from what he called 'Otherworld,' Judge Gamious had assigned both his Chief Guard and his second-in-command to accompany me on my expulsion from his kingdom. The glow from the cavern walls in the region we passed through actually generated some heat. I became quite thirsty as we continued through the long dusty trek, away from the populated areas of Innerland. Even though I was parched the guards would not take pity on me to share any water. However, I did pick up some of their names (and a little about their personalities) from the snatches of conversation I overheard as we continued on our seemingly endless trek.

You need to understand that opinions of my captors are, of course, colored by my perspective, and the fact that I knew that each of them wanted me dead by order of their master. There may have been more to these people than I surmised, but at the time, they seemed pretty shallow to my way of thinking.

Corun, the Second Head Guard (who tried to kill me the day before) seemed like he was trying to suppress the good guy in him. He probably remembered more of his father's teachings than Vocata was ready to admit. I maintain that he was fighting an inward battle; probably between the life he led now, and the life he had been taught to lead by his father. I had some hint of that, young as I was, because of experiences with my own father. I found myself regretting some of my rebellion against Dad, yet at the same time felt glad that I had not violated the basic principles of goodness that I believed he had tried to instill in me. It was apparent that Corun had violated those principles his father had taught him, and he knew it. I didn't think the knowing was making the Second Head Guard happy. I don't know how Corun could have rated his position. Softness and indecision were apparent in his actions. He was not as hardened as his fellow warriors. Once, he was even about to offer me some water, until Atten caught his eye and shook his head warningly.

Atten was one that I had encountered only since this journey. I surmised a great deal about him from observation. He was the Chief Guard over Gamious' flunkies. If Corun seemed to be a little soft or indecisive, this guy was the exact opposite. Being warrior emanated from every pore of his being. I had little doubt that if Atten had been the guard trying to kill me yesterday in the streets of Reach that my story would have ended then. He was completely obedient to Gamious. From the way Atten constantly chided Corun, he had self-appointed himself to be the latter's teacher.

After long hours, we finally took a short break for noonses. My bonds were temporarily removed, and I was allowed a cup of water and a hard-roll to eat. I know it doesn't sound like much. It wasn't; especially when compared with the fare my captors enjoyed. But I had not eaten since noonses the day before, so I savored every drop and bite. Meager though my rations were, I felt strengthened by them.

After about fifteen minutes, my abductors apparently thought me sufficiently strengthened as well. Upon leaving the wagon parked at the side of the trail, one of the guards tied my hands behind my back. He then looped it on another rope to make a kind of leash. I was required to walk the rest of the way that day. While strolling bound, across the uneven landscape, I listened to the guards' jibes and graphic descriptions of the misery I would endure at the hands of the slowlis the following day. This must have been designed to further humiliate me, but it had quite the opposite effect. I could ignore the insults after awhile. And, though tired, I felt invigorated by the walk. It felt good to be physically moving about, rather than lying uncomfortably prone on the bed of a wagon.

We finally reached the end of our journeying for the day. The cavern glow became dim as the guards made camp in the eerie twilight. I was bound tightly (hands and feet again) then pushed into a heavy canvas tent, with only a single guard left to watch the entrance. I was allowed no supper, but more than food, I missed the feel of the cool night breeze that had just begun to blow prior to my being confined in the musty, close feeling tent.

I was tired, but had no desire to sleep. I was delighted because it was the first time that I had been completely alone all day. Well, alone except for the guard at my tent door, but he was already snoring.

Anyway, I had worked over in my mind several different scenarios for my escape. It was time to attempt some of those. I didn't intend to walk willingly into the terrors I had heard described that afternoon. Twice before I had been able to work the bonds loose, even though they felt tight at first. My first object was to see if I could get the ropes loose enough to slip a hand out. When I attempted it, I was successful in getting one hand free on my first try. I was greatly encouraged by my rapid progress. It was but the work of fifteen to twenty minutes later that I was completely free of my bonds.

Everyone seemed to be pretty much out for the night. I could hear just a few voices of men talking quietly, so I allowed myself the luxury of massaging the feeling back into my numbed hands and feet. I didn't want to make any clumsy noises during my escape to alert anyone of my being free. I didn't want to let a numbed foot cause me a misstep in the dark.

The guard at my tent would likely be in deep trouble the next day. He slept soundly enough that it was fairly easy to relieve him of the wooden sheath knife that lay loosely in his belt. The knife was a strange contraption that looked like a flattened cylinder of wood. Most of the guards were equipped with one. I had seen these blades used for many cutting tasks during the course of our walking that day. The cylinder pulled apart at the center to reveal a blade of incredible sharpness. The rear wall of the tent made barely a sound as it sliced open vertically to refresh me with the coolness of the night breeze. The familiar sweet smell of the musk trees was invigorating as I passed from my canvas prison.

So far my plan had worked more efficiently, and more quickly, than I had even hoped. Thanks were due, in part, to the over-tired guard who still lay snoozing at the tent I had just exited. I almost felt sorry for the trouble he would be in come morning. Almost.

I know now that I should have followed my plan to get out of there as fast as I could. However, as I furtively crawled to the edged of the encampment, I heard some voices that made me alter my plans somewhat. Just a few tents to the side of my intended path of escape, I could hear the muffled voices of Corun and Atten in a whispered conference. Being curious, and since everyone else seemed to be sleeping, I crept over to the rear of their tent to hear a little better.

"But you know he is just having the boy killed to rile my father," hissed Corun. I wonder if Corun realized that he had probably merited his rank of leadership for the same reason. He certainly hadn't been given his position because of his ability to lead. It was easy to surmise that from my observations of him earlier that afternoon. It was also fairly obvious that Vocata and Gamious despised one another. I imagine their antagonistic feelings towards one another went back a few cycles, deep as they seemed at each meeting I'd witnessed.

"If it had been any other child, Gamious would have let him go with a good beating," Corun continued. "At the very most, the child would have had just a hand cut off!" How grisly!

Atten's response was slow and measured. "Interesting, to hear you defending the boy. From all accounts, you would have slain him yourself, if not for your father's intervention, son of Vocata."

I could not see Corun's face, but judging by the fierceness of his reply, I could I imagine his features quickly flushing red with anger.

"Do not call me that!" Corun spat contemptuously. "I renounced my relationship to Vocata when I was chosen to serve Gamious as Second Head Guard! It is only Gamious and his purposes that I serve."

"Then why, according to what I hear from some of the other guards who were present," Atten continued in a measured tone, "Why, did you refer to Vocata as 'Father' when you crossed paths with him yesterday?"

"I was caught off guard by him," defended Corun in an embarrassed tone. "Vocata seemed to appear from nowhere. I only saw him as my spear was knocked from the boy's chest! I thought I had already killed the brat, until I saw him get to his feet."

Atten scolded, "You should have killed them both, while you had the chance. It would have made the planned enslavement of the outer areas easier, possibly even allowed it to happen sooner. This half-concocted religion of the Reaches makes it difficult to convince those citizens of trade agreements that will nudge them to serve the desires of Gamious. Right now their total loyalty to Coreterior is hard to achieve, what with their affections divided between their political leader and this mythical 'Deliverer.' However, the longer the Deliverer postpones his return, the easier it is to convince more and more of the populace that their belief in him is just a lot of superficial nonsense. You should have destroyed your father once and for all, Corun, my friend. But even with Vocata still about, if Gamious can score a point against him here and there, the people will believe in your father less and less. Vocata had not power over Gamious to prevent the boy's death. The people will see this inability in Vocata as a weakening." As I listened, I began beginning to despise Atten almost as much as I already abhorred Gamious!

After a moment, Atten continued with his twisted teaching of Vocata's eldest son. "So in a way, Corun, you are right about Gamious having Jef-Re executed to vex your father. But you see, any vexation of Vocata furthers the purposes you have sworn to serve. Remember that. Remember also that Gamious has promised comfortable stations in his new realm to those that serve him faithfully. Better stations by far than what your former family and people will fare at his hands, as they are conscripted to work in his mines."

"I know," replied Corun, "And I want to rise to my proper station in this new order."

It was quiet for a few moments longer. The two Head Guards seemed to be settling down for the night. I was getting ready to crawl off, knowing that I had to get my newfound information to Vocata and his people, in order to warn them of Gamious' intentions.

As I began to leave, Corun's voice quietly broke the silence, causing me another moment's hesitation. "I know this sounds crazy, Atten," he hesitated. "But what if this boy, Jef-Re, is from Otherworld?"

Atten could barely hide the contempt he felt at Corun for asking such a question. "Of course he's from Otherworld, you half-wit. Why do you think we've gone to all of this trouble to make certain he dies? Gamious is aware of the occasional interference of Otherworlders in the affairs of Innerland, but they are not gods. Gamious ran across some ancient records that hinted of a Deliverer in prehistory that actually died at the hands of a slowlis. Yes, a Deliverer who failed! Although stronger than the typical Inlander, it's nice to know Otherworlders are mortal too, eh? It won't matter now after tomorrow anyway. The slowlis will likely have the same appetite for Otherworlders as they do for Inlanders. The subject will likely be academic after the-"

I didn't get to hear the rest of that secret discussion. The coolness of the night air, after the heat of the journey that day, had caused a sneeze to interrupt what Atten was saying. Unfortunately, the sneeze that interrupted him was my own!

Not waiting to see when the two head guards would deduce that it was me that was eavesdropping outside of their tent, I jumped to my feet, and quickly ran in the direction I thought safety lay. It was only after I had run several hundred meters that I realized a fatal mistake; I was running further along the trail we had been following, rather than back the way we had come that day!

I abandoned the idea to turn and follow my intended path back through the camp, because I suddenly heard several yells and incriminations as the men of the campsite came alive to pursue me. My adrenaline worked overtime to keep me just beyond my pursuers. Fortunately, because of the darkness, my pursuers had no idea where I had gone. The mass of guards was not on my tail, but spread several different directions. Though spread out, they had the advantage; while I groped in blackness, they had torches and glow sticks to partially light their paths.

It was terrifying to stumble through the complete unearthly darkness of that night. I eventually had an idea to go off of the main trail and hide in a clump of bushes, hopefully to let my trackers walk on past me. I figured that since the three on my trail were following at such a rapid pace, they might not have actually picked up my tracks. Instead, they may have just been following an assigned direction. My hypothesis proved true; shortly thereafter they came upon my hiding place, and passed on without pausing at the bushes where I lay hidden.

After the three soldiers passed my location, and proceeded several meters into the distance to cross a small stream, an idea occurred to me. It may have been kind of dumb idea, I admit, but it was the best I could manage, given the situation. I wanted to get as far away from the main body of soldiers as I could. These were clearly the only three following this path towards the lair of the slowlis (wherever that was.) If following them got me away from the other guards, then it accomplished my goal. I could make it back to West Reach later. So... I decided to follow them. Not too closely. And quietly!

We walked for hours. It was pretty slow going, and the terrain gradually became rougher, so our progress became even slower. I couldn't see clearly the trackers ahead of me, but enough to occasionally see what they looked like, and note their bumbling antics as they attempted to discover me. The leader was a guy named Ker-Lee. I didn't catch the names of the other two because the leader never called them by name... just slapped them on the head when they did something he thought was stupid. What added more to the humor of the situation was that it was me they searched for, and I had been following them for several hours now!

They clearly disliked their duty, and having to carry it out with one another added to their misery. Even though the landscape slowed us, we probably would have gotten further faster if they hadn't fought among themselves so much. It got to the point that the two followers would duck before Ker-Lee cocked his hand back to slap them. Ker-Lee? Curly- of course! The combination of their leader's bald head, the threesome's continual antics as they searched for me, and the resemblance they bore to three famous Hollywood actors, led me to nickname them Curly, Mo, and Larry.

As the night wore on, the absurd actions of my 'stooge' hunters grew the more comical. They really seemed to think they were following my trail, and all the time I was following them! I might really have had a good time, if it weren't for the recurring thought of how much danger I was in.

-CHAPTER TEN-
A Slowlis Called Iamb

As the cavern walls began to glow with faint light, signaling the early hours of morning, the trio I was following halted beneath a large outcropping of rocks and started to argue anew. Below the rocks where they were standing, was a large grove of musk trees that the path bisected. I silently crept closer, keeping the undergrowth between us, as I attempted to get into a position to hear them.

"I dun't care what Atten ordered us tu du. We're close tu thee slowlis territory, I ken feel et. We'll all get eaten alive uf we dun't turn back nuw!" This from Mo.

"Aye, and we'll get eaten alive by Atten if we return without the boy," countered Ker-Lee, as he slapped Mo on the head. The chubby bald guard I had nicknamed Curly was playing his part well. The argument was almost funny. "We know that he came this way. We saw signs of his passing when we first headed along this trail late last night. It's our duty to find him, and carry out our orders."

"Forget the orders, we could make up a story," suggested Larry. Curly looked at him disgustedly. Undaunted, Larry continued his proposition before Curly could slap him on the back of the head. "We could say... that just as we came upon the boy, a... a... slowlis jumped out and ate him. Yeah, that's it. But since we were older... much older and stronger, we could run faster. Yeah. And we barely escaped with our lives! Gamious has gotta believe that. And then our mission is accomplished. Right?"

Curly and Mo seemed to consider Larry's proposition for a moment or two, then Curly shook his head, and said, "Good idea. Except for one thing... the part about the slowlis. They don't move very fast. That's why they are called slowlis, button head!"

I never got to find out whether they would have accepted Larry's plan or not, because immediately after Curly's objection, just as he was walking over to Larry (presumably to slap him on the head) an enormous beast, longer than a minivan, leaped out of the gully on the far side of the path and swallowed Larry in one gulp! Larry didn't even have a chance to scream. The guards exercised their opportunity to do so however, and ran around making quite a racket. It probably would have been gross, except that there was no blood when Larry was eaten. He was arguing one instant, and gone the next!

I stupidly stepped out onto the path to better see the amazing creature. It was terrifying, but I had never before seen anything like it. I had to get a better look. Curly and Mo ran past me, screaming at the top of their lungs. It was almost comical. I was surprised at how quickly Ker-Lee could run; given his bulk and the shape he appeared to be in. As they brushed past me they didn't even pause in their hasty retreat.

The slowlis (that must have been what the beast was) stalked back and forth across the path, chewing slowly while he contemplated me. I realized then that I should have stayed hidden, but it was the most beautiful creature I had ever seen! At the moment, I was glad to have left my cover to examine it more closely. It looked like a thick serpent, yet with legs.

The body of the creature was covered in plated scales, like a dragon out of legend. Its skin consisted of several beautiful deep green hues, some of which matched the musk trees surrounding us. Its forelegs were larger than its haunches, and muscular like a bulldog. It had four toes on the end of each leg, all ending in mighty claws: three facing forwards, and an opposing center toe behind- sort of like an owl.

Its eyes were catlike and enormous. The shimmering yellow orbs held my gaze as I looked into them. Its stride was feline, its movement fluid. While it examined me, as a tiger might scrutinize its prey, the beast began to glow with a light that came from within, gradually changing its color to an increasingly golden shimmer as the light intensified!

I thought last night that I would follow the guards as a rue. I would escape when I thought they had led me far enough away from the main body of soldiers that I could return back to West Reach unnoticed. I had succeeded, at least in my escape from the guards. But as the glowing slowlis leaped towards me, its gigantic mouth opened to engulf me as it had Larry only moments before, it occurred to me that I might have procrastinated my escape just a little too long.

As the colossal beast leaped, my fascination held me rooted to the spot. I wanted to run as the palace guards had done just moments before. I wanted to fight. I wanted to do something. Those immense orbs that were this monster's eyes stole my ability to move. It was not unlike the power the golden sphere on Corun's breastplate had over me, when he tried to kill me the two days prior. I remembered then the legends I had heard of dragons, how it was said that one could paralyze a man if he looked into its eyes... This was not legend though; this was my reality. I had looked into the creature's eyes, and it still held me transfixed. If I did nothing, my journey among the living would likely soon come to an abrupt end!

The moment before the dreadful beast was upon me, I finally summoned up the resolve to roll to my side into a little clump of musk trees that were prolific in this part of Innerland. As the monster turned to intercept me, I snapped off a fair-sized branch at waist level from a nearby tree. The stick was a little less than a meter in length. I brought it around in a sweeping arc, and plastered the limb hard across my attacker's enormous left eye.

The slowlis stopped, blinked once, and then jumped forward again, this time hitting me and knocking me off balance. The gigantic monster then pinned me to the ground with one enormous paw. Though I was held firmly on the ground, I was not crushed, and still breathed freely, albeit rapidly. The slowlis examined me closely.

He's probably deciding whether to eat me whole, or in bites, I grimly thought. Getting a feel for the size of this beast up close I realized just how futile my defense had been. It was roughly the size and length of a small school bus, though not as clumsy or bulky. Still, I thought, If I am to meet my end this way, at least I know I have tried. It was the most consolation I could muster at the time. I escaped the guards, only to walk right into the fate they had originally intended for me!

I squinted as I gazed upward at this immense glowing beast. Its descending maw opened wide above my head. Looking closer I saw rows upon rows of barbed teeth. My stomach nearly lurched from the fetid smell of its breath. Though I knew at this point it was useless, I still continued to struggle under the abomination's unyielding grasp. Then, when its teeth were mere centimeters from my face, the slowlis pulled back, drooled, and fell on its side making deep guttural roars.

[Hnaaaaa. Hnaaaaa. Hnaaaaa.]

It was laughing! It was laughing?

My first thought was that the thing was toying with me, as a cat with a mouse. Surprised by this turn of events, and not knowing what else to do, I rolled to the side, recovered my stick and jumped back into a defensive stance. For an uncomfortable minute or so the slowlis continued to roll on the ground, clutching its sides as it repeated its annoying guttural laugh.

[Hnaaaaa. Hnaaaaa. Hnaaaaa.]

Finally, after leveling a dozen saplings by its gyrations, the creature regained its footing and approached me. From the curvature of its mouth, I think it was smiling!

[You passed Stripling. Hnaaaaa. Hnaaaaa. You passed.]

The bulbous lips of the creature did not move, yet I heard its voice in my mind as clearly as if it had spoken aloud.

"You can... *speak?*" I half asked, half stated.

[After a manner.] The beast replied. [It is speech you hear in your mind. You understand my speech through impressions on your thoughts.]

"It bothers me to be talked to like this," I stammered, surprised at my sudden boldness. "Vocata did the same thing to me. Stop it now!"

"Iaay kuhn taalk wit ta muuth lik yuu if ta lik mew tuu," replied the slowlis; this time opening its mouth wide while it slowly formed the sounds of each individual syllable. The speech was not very understandable, and its breath was unbearable. I clutched my mouth to keep from vomiting, and stumbled backward a couple of steps.

"On second thought, the telepathy will be just fine," I retorted, still feeling nauseous from its breath, and not really feeling a desire to see those teeth any longer. I guess mind-communication had its place after all.

[I understand.] It replied, this time within my thoughts again. [Others I have talked with have also preferred communicating in this way, after experiencing the alternative. Even other slowlis. Is there anything else?]

"Well. The fluids surrounding you are very bright. It's uncomfortable to look at you," I continued, as I looked to the side and shielded my eyes.

[Sorry about that. This I can control too.] The ancient slowlis closed its eyes as if concentrating deeply. After a few moments of silence the light surrounding it began to dim. Soon its skin turned back to many shades of green, as when I had first seen it. I still found the beauty of the beast before me to be completely captivating.

I began to feel calmer in the presence of the slowlis. I even sensed that it was a he. There was more going on between our minds than just the words I could identify. Impressions deeper than conscious thought were rapidly occurring within my brain. Soon my fear of being destroyed ebbed, and I felt comforted. Somehow I knew that I was not in any danger from Iamb. Iamb. That was his name. Suddenly I knew his name as if it had been part of my knowledge all along.

"Thank you, Iamb," I offered. "Why did you not destroy me as Vocata and the others claimed you would?"

[Because you are a Deliverer. Besides, even Vocata can be mistaken, on occasion.]

"Please..." I muttered in shock. A new panic, different from that I had felt a moment ago, began to well up inside of me. Then I stood silently for a long moment. Rousing up additional courage, I implored the giant further, "I am not from here... how can I be a... Deliverer?"

[Silence inside for now, Jeff,] the slowlis stated slowly and directly. [You will understand in time. You will also stay with me. How long? I know not. For what? I will tell you, in part. As you know, I am called Iamb. I am to teach you, as I taught the Deliverer before you. I have waited long for your coming. Besides cutting the tunnels in cycles past, this is my purpose. Come.]

Iamb wheeled his great mass around, with a speed that I again found surprising, and shuffled away. He moved fast, even considering the speed with which he attacked and ate Larry. His shuffling could be called such only because of how awkward it looked to me. His continually rapid pace belied his tremendous bulk, and I had to exert myself to follow in a run rather than a walk. I had thought being a slowlis might mean he would move slow or something. I think the guards had too. Considering the recent attack, and the foot race we were now engaged in, Iamb was anything but slow.

The only reason why I chose to follow, rather than flee (as the Judge's minions had) was a continued feeling of trust that emanated from this big eyed lizard. I was beginning to trust my inner feelings more than I used to. It was those feelings, I remembered, that had allowed me to trust Vocata. They had also warned me about the character of the Great Center Judge upon our first meeting. Besides, I had a pretty good idea what would happen to me at the hands of Gamious and his friends. I had already fared much better with this creature. Aside from his breath, Iamb wasn't all that bad.

Bet Gamious won't try to mess with me while I'm with Iamb, I thought to myself as we forded a small river.

[Bet you are right, Jeff,] replied Iamb within my mind.

As we walked for the rest of that day, I gradually began to get used to the idea of my thoughts being an open book to this creature. It didn't appear that he would turn the mind reading off as Vocata had done.

-CHAPTER ELEVEN-
Tutored by a Beast

My journey with the slowlis, called Iamb, continued for three days. We slept when the caverns grew too dark for me to see, and then we walked when they began their glow each morning. Iamb said he could have glowed at night to show our way, but I insisted I needed some rest. As we walked, I reflected back on my first journey. It now seemed ages ago that after following Tabob for a couple of hours I felt exhausted. That first trek seemed like a leisurely walk compared with the journey we now undertook. During this trek I didn't even have the delusion of waking up from a dream into a well-rested morning. Still, though the pace was quick, all the walking I had done over the last several weeks allowed me to keep up with Iamb pretty well.

Many of the tunnels and caverns looked similar to others I had traversed. Similar plant and animal life were to be found in each. I even noticed a small colony of glibs in a lone stand of trees. Hearing the familiar, "Cheee cheee cheeeeee," caused me to feel homesick for Pounce and Mib. Though I had been away from them for just a couple of days, I missed them terribly. My constant association with my friends these past weeks was something I grew to expect. Being away from them caused me to feel a great void that could only be filled by their companionship. I wondered if they were safe from the treachery of Gamious. His two chief guards had talked of his plans to enslave the Inlanders for some mining operation. I hoped I might make the citizens of West Reach aware of the Center Judge's plans so they could prevent their occurrence somehow. Iamb, sensing my concern, impressed upon my mind the feeling that my companions were alright. I appreciated his concern, and was grateful for the comfort he offered to my troubled thoughts. However, I still continued to worry about Mib and the others, as I was once again gradually left to my own thoughts.

Eventually, the caverns and tunnels began to open up more. As they did, I noticed less and less of the now familiar plant and animal life that I had become used to since staying with Vocata and his family. I also began to discern a different light source from up in the distance. The coloration seemed strangely familiar, yet foreign to what I had become accustomed to. A little farther, and we emerged into the world as I remembered, but had not seen for weeks. We were above ground!

I thought gleefully at first, *I am home!* But those thoughts were soon dashed as I realized that this new environment looked little like the Earth I remembered. Nor did it resemble Innerland. Not worrying now whether I lost Iamb's lead, I sank down dejectedly under the edge of a bright green and yellow forest of spiny trees the color of lichen. The trunks were about half a meter to a meter in width. Most of the older trees seemed to reach about twenty to thirty meters in height.

[Come Deliverer. You are time wasting.] The slowlis ambled back where he saw me sitting. [Up on my back. Now! We are in open air. No danger of scraping you off on a bit of unfinished meal-rock. Now we can move faster!]

Faster? I thought, as I reflected on the pace we had maintained for the last couple of days. *I'm glad you're going to be doing the walking, Iamb.*

I gratefully sank into the hollow at the back of his neck and basked in the glow of a life-giving sun. I had forgotten how much I had missed open air. The regular pace of Iamb's run, and the secure feeling of riding, curled safely in the folds of his neck, soon lulled me to a much-earned sleep. I don't even remember dreaming while I dozed during the remainder of our journey that day.

* * *

Iamb became my teacher and guide to this new realm, called simply, 'Outside.' An accurate if not creative description of where we now were. The strangest thing that I noticed about Outside was that it never got dark! The sun in that sky stayed in the exact same position at all times. Surprisingly, it didn't cause the environment to be extremely hot; it was just comfortably warm. There were occasional breezes that cooled the surface as well. If the plants seemed plentiful in Innerland, they looked sparse compared to the overwhelming amount of vegetation I witnessed on the surface.

You may wonder how I knew if it was day or night, especially since the sun was always up. My own internal body clock told me when it was time to sleep, and so I was on a pretty normal schedule;

at least as near as I could tell. The vegetation was thick enough that for the times I desired sleep, I could duck under a stand of trees, and the shade would make it as dark as early evening. Most of the time though, evening was accompanied by cloud-cover, which further darkened the land. I had no problem sleeping under the endless canopy of trees. The foliage also provided foods aplenty to satiate my appetite. Though I might have liked some variation in my diet, I didn't go hungry the entire time I ate the fruits and nuts that grew in the land of Outside. After eating nothing but fruits and nuts for a couple of days though, I began to long for a hamburger and fries. However, that was more out of old habit than need.

Some of the animals were the same kind as had been in Innerland. Still, most were green, of course. My second day up, I even ran across another small colony of glibs chattering in the treetops. These intelligent little creatures had ventured further than the Inlanders had dared to go. Seeing them made me homesick again for my pet glib, Pounce, and the friends I had made while in Innerland. This loneliness caused me not to spend much more time looking at the glibs that day. I soon after wandered off to find Iamb, and accomplish my day's lessons.

* * *

Through Iamb's teachings, I eventually came to understand much more about the workings of Innerland and Outside. The glowing phosphorescence painted on the cavern walls (which gave Innerland its day-night cycle) was a secretion from the many slowlis who had made the tunnels and caverns. This much I knew from what Vocata had told me. What I learned more about it though was that the slowlis were an ancient race that predated the arrival of Inlanders. It had taken probably millions of cycles for the myriad of slowlis to eat the tunnels, and for the subsequent environment to establish itself and flourish. When the slowlis ate the rock ('meal-rock,' Iamb called it) their bodies converted the mass into energy. Part of that energy took the form of a secretion that rubbed off the slowlis and onto the cavern walls. I didn't quite understand why it glowed in day/night cycles as it did, but it came in handy, as the glow of the walls was what the Inlanders reckoned their days by.

Iamb's teachings centered mainly on the history of another Deliverer; the one that had come before me. I didn't fully understand the title of Deliverer, but it was what Iamb frequently referred to me as, so I became used to being called by that title. I surmised that a Deliverer came to this world every time the people were in great need, and could be either male or female. I was one of countless other Deliverers that had come previously. Iamb predicted that after me, there would likely be others. Their coming had always been linked to a Stone of Recognition, an artifact out of dim antiquity. As Vocata had been, Iamb was concerned that I didn't have the Stone. After awhile though, he sloughed it off and said that great emotion could probably have caused the transition that had brought me here, since I seemed the one currently destined to fill the role. I gathered the Stone he referred to was more a part of the tradition, and gave previous Deliverers control over when they came (rather than in the middle of a conversation, as with me.) Even though he said I'd likely manage fine without the Stone, I was curious to see it. I wondered also why I was apparently the first Deliverer to be here without the Stone of Recognition.

Though he talked a lot, some things Iamb was a little secretive about. For example, I would frequently ask what I was supposed to deliver the Inlanders from. Iamb would simply smile and say, [You will know when the time comes.] That was not a great comfort to me. True, at home I had never really prepared for most of my school assignments. However, when it was something really important, like an art assignment, I would be prepared. This felt important. I wanted to be more prepared for whatever it was I was supposed to accomplish here. I felt that I wanted to do it right, and live up to the standard that others had set before me.

[All of the others worried too,] reminded Iamb when I got really stressed. [And like them, you will succeed.] Though not total, it was still some reassurance, coming from him.

Though Iamb told me briefly about many Deliverers, he concentrated mostly on the last one. Whenever Iamb would begin to speak of him, he would pause, give me a long and searching look, and then proceed to tell me of how that Deliverer had accomplished the feat of moving the people away from the problems they faced about three hundred cycles ago. Iamb had been chosen to be that particular Deliverer's teacher also, as he had now been elected by the other slowlis to be mine. I guess the Inlanders used to live Outside, until the orbit of their planet took them to a position out of direct sunlight. Their world became cold and began to die. The last Deliverer led the Terrainians (they didn't used to call themselves Inlanders) below ground to the environment created in part by the race of slowlis. Terrainians. Sounded like something out of a comic book!

"Why didn't the Terrainians just migrate to the other side of the planet?" I asked my tutor. It seemed a pretty logical idea to me.

[The distance on the surface is far too great. Even the great speed of a slowlis could not have made the trek back to light by the time the people realized their problem.]

"How does it happen that the surface is so alive now?" I asked.

[This part of our world has again turned to face our sun, thus allowing life. The flora you see will continue to flourish for many hundreds of cycles yet. The life will last until the rotation of our planet again takes us into the dark time.]

I once asked Iamb what the name of this former Deliverer was. I was understandably curious, since he talked of him so much. Iamb just stared at me... long and searchingly. Then, ignoring the question, he continued with his stories. I guessed that it wasn't proper to ask the name of that Deliverer. The people (and other creatures, like the slowlis) seemed to hold him in great awe and respect. Perhaps part of that respect mandated that they not refer to him by name.

The prior Deliverer eventually fell in love with a beautiful Inlander woman. After setting up the society and government of Inland, he married the woman, and took her to live with him in his reality on Earth. He used the Stone of Recognition to transport them both. A marriage between a Deliverer and an Inlander had never happened in all of the history of this people before that point. No one saw or heard from either of them for many, many cycles.

Then, about eighty cycles ago, the Deliverer and his bride returned. They both had aged only a few cycles, even though approximately two hundred and twenty cycles had passed in Innerland. After living several years in Earth time, his bride began to grow ill until she thought she would die if they didn't return to Inland. Back at West Reach, she seemed to heal and grow healthy once again, so they decided to remain. The Deliverer would have been immortal for as long as he dwelt in Innerland, which he did for several cycles. Iamb claimed that the entire time he lived here he never aged the cycle of a day, even though his wife grew steadily older.

After several more cycles, it was discovered that his bride was with child. Shortly thereafter she gave birth to a boy-child. That boy was Vocata, the father of Tabob and Mib! Vocata had to stay with the mother and the Inlanders for it was believed that since they had both been born in this world that they would both have to stay here, or risk dying if they returned to Earth. They all three continued as a family for a couple of cycles, enjoying the peace and prosperity of Innerland. Then, one cycle, the Deliverer returned to his world. Iamb said he did not know the reason why the man chose to leave. Apparently there was some pressing business left there that he and his bride both agreed he should return for. The Deliverer didn't return to Inland until eight cycles later. He found his wife had died two cycles previous to his return. Vocata was then approaching the age of ten. The Deliverer was devastated.

"But why did he wait eight cycles to return, if he loved his wife and son so much?" I asked angrily. He was becoming my hero, and this part of the story didn't sit well with me.

[He did not. He came the very next day, according to his world's reckoning of time,] replied Iamb. [There is a differential of time between our worlds. Little predictability exists even in this. The first time the Deliverer left he spent six or seven years in his world with his wife. Yet over two hundred cycles had passed by our reckoning. The third time he returned, after leaving his wife and young son, by his reckoning he had been gone only overnight. However, eight cycles had passed according to our perspective.]

"So he hadn't really stayed away for eight cycles after all," I said, greatly relieved that my new hero wasn't some hypocrite who had abandoned his wife and son.

[No,] countered Iamb, [But the effect was the same. And his bride never knew that he hadn't just gone off and deserted her and their toddler, Vocata. The Deliverer came back several times after that to see his son. Each was at eight cycle intervals. Though the length of time to the deliverer varied from a mere moment to a couple of days. The Deliverer never returned after seeing a nearly fifty cycle old Vocata; the son had aged more than the father! I had never seen a man so broken. It saddened me to see him suffering, especially one who had done so much good for so many others. That was nearly thirty-two cycles past. Each eight cycles Vocata or one of his sons watched the gate, waiting for his return. Vocata is over eighty cycles old. Though extremely robust (even for an Inlander) he is, as you know, a very old man. He always believed his father would again return. He did not.]

"What was that Deliverer's name?" I asked again, fearing that I already knew Iamb would just stare at me as he had every other time that I had asked this over the last several days.

Iamb's response was a little different this time though. In addition to the deep and thoughtful stare, a bit of moisture trickled from his immense right eye. I learned, as I gazed at him then, that a slowlis could cry. I hadn't expected a response such as that.

"He must have been very dear to you," I awkwardly said, trying to cover over this sudden mood change by further conversation.

The slowlis remained speechless for a time, staring deeply at me, as if searching for something. After a few more moments, Iamb turned, characteristic for the first time of his name, and slowly sauntered off in the direction of the deep forest.

-CHAPTER TWELVE-
Gum-Paste, Again!

Like Mib, Iamb was willing to answer many of my questions. Between them, I felt that I knew more about Innerland's culture than I did about U.S. History. Maybe it was the way they taught me. I couldn't always seem to access the information from books that my teachers assigned me, however, the hands-on lessons always stayed with me. The last few months as a visitor to this world had been very hands-on!

If Iamb bore a similarity to Mib in showing a willingness to answer many of my questions, he also bore a contrasting likeness to Vocata, in at least one aspect: He was evasive about a great number of things. Additionally, Iamb made me work for many of the answers I eventually nudged out of him.

"Why did my asking you about the former Deliverer cause you to weep the other day?"

[You will understand in time, Jeff.]

"How did Vocata know my name? He would never tell me."

[You will understand in time, Jeff.]

"You have taught me many things about how the previous Deliverer helped the people now called Inlanders. How am I supposed to help them by my being here?"

You guessed it. Iamb simply replied, [You will understand in time, Jeff.]

Frustrated, after having many such dead-end conversations, I'm afraid my patience finally lagged one day. "Why must you always answer my most important questions with a put off, Iamb?"

[You will understand in time, Jeff.]

I steeled the great slowlis with the iciest teacher-glare I could muster. Believe me, I had seen some stern looks used on me during my career as a student. Iamb smiled, showed all of his teeth, and gave me just a hint of that fatal breath.

He then added, [Jeff. If I were to tell you the entire reason you were here, you would do one of two things. Either you would not believe me, or you would think me crazy.]

[And perhaps a third alternative,] he added, after probing me with his gaze for a while longer. [You would forget the purpose if I simply told you. All of the information that I give you, you have for a time. Information that is only temporarily needful, I have freely given you. But the knowledge that you get for yourself, that which really matters, it is yours; you will keep it for always. Do you understand my meaning?]

I had been with Iamb for several days, and had gotten used to the mind-communication and his manner of teaching. I had thought that I was beginning to understand many things. But I didn't quite get his meaning in this regard. "No," I confessed, "I don't quite follow you, big fellow."

[Let me illustrate. You have maintained that Gamious is an evil man. Who told you that he was evil?]

"Why Mib and Vocata both warned... No- I see what you mean," I said suddenly. That was something I learned through experience. The knowledge I had of him, and his evil intentions towards me, strengthened my resolve to expose the plans that I had overheard his guards discussing the night of my escape. If I had only been told that he was a no-good person, I would not likely be as eager to reveal his treachery to the Inlanders of West Reach. Maybe Iamb wasn't such a crazy old lizard after all.

[You will understand in time, Jeff. And as you do, the knowledge will be yours. If I were to simply outline what you were to do, I would (in a very real sense) be robbing you of that which it is your right to discover. In addition to your growth by gaining knowledge, it will be of more worth to you because it will be you who are the one to uncover the knowledge you need. I believe that the 'Knowing' you so need, will come to you of its own accord, and by your seeking it. The experiences you have by searching your purpose out will assist you in using the knowledge you find in a wise manner.]

We shared silence for several long moments. As I sat, wrapped in the warmth of the ever-present sun, I believed in the words of Iamb; the strange lizard-like beast that had the wisdom of ages. I was glad he had deemed to teach me, and I believed his words were true.

After a little more time had lapsed, Iamb broke the silence. [The time has come for your return, Deliverer. Come. There are a few things yet that I may tell you. I have some items for you that may help you in your journeying as well.]

I followed Iamb through dense undergrowth, to a large, archaic looking stone structure that I had not noticed during my several wanderings these past days. Carvings similar to those I had seen in Innerland graced the posts of the doors. If the etchings had also once been colored, the pigments had long since been washed away. These were the ruins of the Terrainians. I felt somewhat irreverent trespassing here, knowing that these buildings had not been disturbed for three hundred cycles. But I was also excited to see what lay inside. Iamb allowed himself to glow softly as we entered the otherwise stygian blackness of the antechamber he led me within. My friend, the flashlight, came in handy in this darkened chamber. Nudging aside a stone slab atop the table in the center of the room, Iamb showed me some artifacts that he indicated I was to take.

"These belonged to the last Deliverer, didn't they?"

Iamb nodded affirmatively.

Reaching in, I reverently removed the few objects. Sitting down on the cold stone floor of the chamber, I spread the artifacts out so as to examine them more closely.

[He, the Deliverer last, anticipated your coming one day. He left these here in preparation for you. It is good to see his purpose fulfilled full-circle.]

Opening a small tube revealed a map. It clearly marked the paths back to Innerland, the main entrance I had come through, as well as several antiquated settlements Outside. Good. Now I could find my way back. This map was not difficult to discern because map reading was the other thing besides knot tying that I had paid attention to during my short stint with the Boy Scouts; I only hoped I would not be required to build a fire without matches.

The next object I examined resembled the wooden sheath knife attached to my belt that I had relieved from the guard (during my escape from Gamious' men) last week. This was also a flattened cylinder of wood, but the length was from my thigh to my ankle. I was not surprised to find a blade when I pulled both halves of the cylinder apart. What did surprise me were the intricately beautiful etchings in the blade. As much as the Inlanders were wood-smiths now, it appeared that their ancestors, the Terrainians, had been adept stone and metal-smiths. The wooden scabbard had leather thongs to carry it with. I slipped it over my shoulders. I was amazed that the wood and the leather could remain so preserved after three hundred cycles. Perhaps it had been placed here on the Deliverer's most recent visit, only thirty-two cycles past.

I had difficulty sensing the logic of the third item, but I put it in my satchel nonetheless. It was a small coin with oriental writing on it. The coin had a square hole cut from the center. I vaguely remembered having seen some of these when younger, but I didn't remember where. It was not from Innerland. It was from my world!

There was also a brown leather book, complete with ornate brass hinges and a hasp. It looked like a journal! I hurried to open it, eager to read from what I thought would be the Deliverer's words. Iamb had other ideas, however. He knocked the book from my grasp and re-deposited it in the stone container. He said I would have time to read it later, whenever that would be. As he closed the slab I wished that I had been faster; At least quick enough to see a signature anyway.

It was difficult to say goodbye to Iamb. I agreed to only after he assured me that we would meet again. However, it troubled me that he would not say when. The map made it easy enough to find my way back. I came carefully, heeding the final warnings of Iamb. Though it had been almost two weeks since my escape, Iamb thought that some of Gamious' people might still be on the lookout for me.

I spent the first night back in the caverns of Innerland with no incident. As I awoke the following morning I felt happy to be back. Funny, but I had missed this place the last week or so, just like I had missed above ground when being within Innerland before. I enjoyed walking at a more leisurely pace than when I had first traversed this area with Iamb several days previously.

The thick canopy of the overhanging trees wove a moving rooftop of green splendor, as the day grew steadily older. It was one of the few times I had been alone in this land. It gave me time to think about why I was here, and how I might help this people. Iamb said to trust my feelings, so I tried to. The feelings I had though were strange. I felt that perhaps I was to tell the others about Outside. Although the environment above was rich and beautiful, I had also found much of Innerland to be so, at least in West Reach. I couldn't find any logical justification for my impressions that might influence any Reach dwellers to want to leave their already beautiful surroundings. Then I remembered the apparent squalor I had witnessed on the outskirts of Coreterior. We had passed through the area at such a rapid speed that I had very few images of it in my memory. What was there though showed a bleakness that contrasted roughly to this bounteous land, and the overwhelming abundance I had witnessed Outside. I especially thought about the lone, hungry looking child I saw as the carriage whistled past the slums on the way to my trial. I thought about it long as I made camp the second night.

    Two mornings later, about an hour after I'd broken camp, I came upon the fringes of the lands of Coreterior. Far beyond the river I was about to cross, on the very horizon, I could just make out the pillars of the palace. More evident to me because of my closer examination was the squalor surrounding that polished edifice. It was not fair, the way the general populace of Coreterior eked out a survival in comparison to the opulent living of the Great Center Judge. I couldn't believe that other Inlanders could be blinded into following that rascal Gamious.

    As I squinted to get an idea of the distance to the palace, trying to get a better bearing as to my location on the map, I heard two voices conversing in low tones close by. I carefully peeked around the edge of an outcropping of rocks to see if I could tell who was there. I was about five kilometers in from where Atten and Corun's group had made camp the night I had escaped. I stopped abruptly as I recognized two of the Judge's guards: Curly and Mo, the remaining pair from the ill-fated trio that had followed me that same night. Though it was early in the day cycle, I figured that it would be easy enough to slip by them as I had done before. I guessed wrong. The guards were aware of me before I had passed even ten meters!

    One thing was certain; after quickly swimming a small river that lay in my path, I did better in our foot race wearing my basketball shoes, than those guys did in their leather sandals. I easily outdistanced them, even wearing waterlogged shoes. Then, using the information on the map, I bypassed the longer route that would have taken me through Coreterior, and cut a couple of hours off of the return trip towards West Reach. After traveling through several small outlying towns and villages, I ended up many hours later coming upon the city of Highland. Judging from the distance on the map, I should be able to make West Reach by late that evening, or early the next day.

Thinking back, I should have been more careful than to come down one of the main walkways of the city. The map had helped me find a quicker way back, but these guys had grown up here. Sitting in front of a tavern, Curly and Mo seemed to be waiting for me as I rounded a corner!

The race was on again. I fairly easily began to outdistance them a second time. As I rounded yet another street corner I heard one of my pursuers, the one I had nicknamed Mo, make a remark to Curly about something being up ahead. His buddy laughed, despite his puffing to keep up. They may have thought they had gotten me, but I wasn't winded yet. After the conditioning my body had received from my journeying in this world, I believed I could beat them in this race. I was glad that it was still early enough in the day that there were not many people about; otherwise the guards might have been assisted by others in the city.

Coming around yet another corner I realized the reason for the two guards' cocky attitude: painted along the path ahead of me, from wall to wall, was about eleven meters of gum paste. This was the same natural adhesive Mib had shown me my second day here. I recalled that it was used in construction to fasten building pieces and hold down walkways. I also remembered that there was really no solvent for it. The tip of my right finger tingled as I thought back on having to have my finger pried off the wall when I touched some of the messy glop.

So I had come across a construction site. I didn't see any workers as I abruptly halted just short of stumbling headlong into a sticky situation. Gamious' two flunkies were almost upon me. I could hear their labored breathing as they approached. I had to act fast or be taken. I knew how I'd fare at their hands if they caught up with me.

Thinking feverishly, I came up with an idea that I thought might get me out of this. I bent down to loosen my shoelaces, backed up a few paces, and then took a running jump lengthwise along the path of the paste! Time switched to slow motion as I became airborne and an eternity later landed hard on my right foot. Not pausing (so I could maintain my momentum) I jumped from my first footing to my left foot, leaving my sneaker adhered to the road's surface. After my left shoe stuck fast, still hurtling forward, I landed on my right stocking.

This was the part of my plan that I especially hoped wasn't in error. I didn't know which would be worse, meeting my fate at the hands of the Great Judge, or having the sole of my foot ripped off to get me free of the glop. Fortunately I didn't have to make that choice as my right foot came cleanly out of my loose (and by this time crusty) stocking.

On to my left foot, and jump... Just short of my goal, the ball of my right foot stuck securely on the very edge of the paste! The momentum of my jumping carried my body in a hard lurch forward onto the rock solid road. Adding injury to my insult, this caused me to twist my still attached ankle in the process.

The guards had arrived in time enough to see my antics as I attempted to escape. Curly and Mo were laughing quite heartily as I made the decision between loosing the sole of my foot and facing their master. My foot lost the contest. Calling forth reserves I didn't know I had, I reached down with both hands and pulled my foot loose with one wrenching motion. The sound and feel of my tearing skin nearly made me retch, but I was free. Trying to ignore the pain, I hobble-ran to Vocata's house in the center of West Reach. The gaping mouthed guards stood stupefied, shocked to the point that they didn't even think to fire off a volley of arrows.

I knew, despite the overwhelming sickness and pain I was feeling, that if I could just make it to Vocata's house everything would be OK. He always knew what to say and do in the past. As I slowly approached West Reach in the dim twilight, I hoped my trust in Vocata was as well founded as my distrust of Gamious and his men had proven to be.

-CHAPTER THIRTEEN-
Familiar Tunnels

It was slow going back to West Reach, what with the ball of my foot raw and in pain. The night had already turned inky when I emerged from the blackness of the musk tree forest surrounding the village. I didn't see any sign of the two guards, Curly and Mo, who had been so hot on my tail in Highland. At first I took this as a good sign; perhaps even with my wounded foot I made better time than I thought. But then I realized that it might just have just given them time to alert others who may be out looking for me, in which case I would not be so fortunate. I determined to approach the sleeping village with greater caution than I had used coming into Highland.

About thirty minutes after sighting the dim lights of the little Reach town, I approached the lane on which Vocata and his family made their ancestral residence. I came slowly, partly from a desire to approach with stealth, and partly because my foot ached with a raw pain from losing a few layers of skin. I kept to the shadows, as the ball of my foot continued its ceaseless throbbing.

A few houses up the street from Vocata's home, a slight movement from the shadows on the other side caused me to freeze in place. I immediately took cover behind a refuse pile on the street corner. It was good that I had, because no sooner had I dropped out of sight than a beam of light probed searchingly in my direction. Whoever it was (and I guessed it was one of the judge's guards) had been pretty smart. They had covered a slowlis bone in thick cloth, and unsheathed it; kind of like turning on a flashlight or uncovering a lantern. Satisfied that no one was there after several passes with the beam, the unidentified guard again doused the light. I didn't think I had made any noise. I would have to exercise even more caution than I thought I was using.

It was a cinch that I would not be able to approach from Vocata's front door. I would have to alert his family quietly too so as not to cause any lights to come on- I had a feeling that the guards would take any glow from within as a sign that I had penetrated their defenses. *Mib*. I could try to approach through her room. If I could alert her without alarming her I think I could get safely off of the streets. Keeping in the darkest shadow, I crawled on my belly behind the houses and off of the street. For a few moments I felt tremendous relief at being off of my aching foot. The two yards over were pretty easy to negotiate, and soon I was crouched at the foot of the flower trellis that ran up the wall between Mib's room and the room I had occupied. My head was swimming from the pain I felt. A throbbing headache had become a familiar companion since the first hour out of Highland. Fighting to keep conscious, I sluggishly extended my tired hands inch over agonizing inch as I ascended the latticework while dragging my useless foot behind me. It seemed like hours later that I finally arrived at the third story of the structure. I was grateful that Mib had left her window open, and so far I had noticed no other movement from my cursory checks of the surrounding area.

After pulling the shutter slowly open a little more, I carefully climbed to the windowsill. Balanced on my belly, about as much in Mib's room as I was still out, I heard a low menacing growl. *Pounce!* As the growl in the room continued to intensify in volume, I noticed two figures stealthily moving in from the distance below me outside.

"Who's there?" A sleepy Mib questioned. "Speak, or I'll call for my father..."

The growling continued to get louder.

Pounce, I thought, *It's me, Jeff. Be quiet little friend!*

Perhaps it was habit from all the mind-communication Iamb had used in teaching me the past several days. Perhaps I sent the message in my thoughts out of a desire to be quiet in case those were guards approaching nearer below me. Perhaps it was some latent instinct. Whatever it was, the message was received, and the growling turned into a purring that I had heard only a few times before from our pet glib.

"Jeff?" queried Mib.

Help me.

As I began to fall, Mib bolted from under her comforter, grabbed my extended hand, and pulled me roughly to her floor. Never had pain felt so good, as did my face hitting the hardwood surface of her bedroom floor that night. *Safety.* Mib didn't pause to see if I was alright though, instead she rushed to the window, threw open the second shutter, and screamed, "Who's outside of my window? Leave, or I will call the City Guards on you!"

I wished I could have seen the expression on the Judge Guard's faces as they beat a hasty retreat! I'm sure it was a turn of events from what they had expected. Judging from her leisurely return, Mib's rue worked. Hopefully my pursuers didn't know I was in the house.

"Good thinking, Mib..." I congratulated, as I lapsed into unconsciousness.

* * *

I awoke beneath a downy quilt. The air in the room was cool. First light was just coming in the three windows on the side of my room. I felt like snuggling further down into the bed awhile. I was exhausted. The mattress was soft; I sunk into it. The pillow was a fluffy and familiar friend. For some reason, my right foot ached. I was a little disoriented.

As I turned over to get some more shut-eye, I was interrupted in my revelry by a tell-tale yip, and suddenly my vision was blotted out by a leathery green glib. Pounce! I sat up in bed, wincing as I pulled against the bandages my foot was wrapped in. Vocata was seated comfortably at the foot of my bed.

"Welcome back to the land of the living, Jeff. That's a nasty wound you've got. Tabob would be disappointed to know that you've been playing around gum-paste again."

I smiled at this sage old man, happy to awake in familiar surroundings. Then suddenly, I remembered Gamious' guards!

"They are gone. For now, anyway," assured Vocata. "Come. Let's get you dressed and down to break your fast." I grabbed my things, including the artifacts that Iamb had given me, and followed my benefactor down to the eatery

It was good to taste meat again, even if it had the same green tinge that most of the animals had around here. Miyab's cooking was even better than I remembered it. Vocata explained what had happened while I had been gone. Tabob had followed his older brother and Atten, intent on spiriting me out of their camp that first night.

"He said that when he got to the tent in which you were being held, that all he found was a sleepy guard. And a rent in the side of the canvas wall big enough for a person to have escaped through," explained Vocata. I smiled inwardly as I reflected upon what I thought had begun as a pretty good escape. Vocata continued, "Tabob tried to find you, to lead you back to West Reach, but shortly thereafter the camp erupted into chaos and he retreated in order to keep from being identified. Tabob said he found your trail later, as well as that of three soldiers who tracked you. He then told me something that I did not believe..."

Vocata looked at me, waiting for me to explain. More than waiting, he expected an explanation. Before I began, I reflected on the fact that I was glad he had made good on his promise of trying to rescue me.

So, I explained what had happened from my perspective. My narration included highlights from the sleeping guard and the stolen knife, to my sneeze that alerted the camp, and my trailing the guards who thought they tracked me. Mib laughed at me for sneezing, then we all started laughing. It did seem kind of funny, now. It was good to be with my adopted family again. I was getting comfortable thinking of them as family.

I then related the details I had overheard about Gamious and his plans to enslave the Reaches. Vocata took especial note of that, and I could almost see his mind working as he processed the new information. I finally got to the part of my story about the slowlis. Though Vocata had relished the information that exposed Gamious as a traitor, I could tell that this was the part of my narration he had been impatient to hear. I explained how I had gone the wrong way when escaping (having gotten turned around in the darkness) and how that later the slowlis attacked the three guards, leaving two.

"You saw a live slowlis?" Mib asked in amazement.

I nodded affirmatively, and then continued. "The beast feigned an attack on me too, until the guards departed, then he spoke to me."

"Tabob said that you followed willingly, " stated Vocata.

I again nodded. They all stopped eating to stare at me.

"How did you escape from the monstrosity?" queried Vocata.

"I didn't." A simultaneous gasp arose from the small assembly. "I have lived with him these past days, learning from him about my mission as the Deliverer." As my three friends gazed on in shocked amazement, I produced the artifacts given me by the slowlis. When I showed the sword of the Deliverer to Vocata, a look of even more profound amazement than I had thought possible crossed his features.

"That... was... my father's sword," he stuttered while his mouth dropped open.

"I know," I replied. Then added, "The last Deliverer."

Mib and Miyab in turn looked at Vocata. I took it that this information was a revelation to them about their father and mate. Vocata meekly smiled an acknowledgement, and then reverently took the sword from me as I offered it to him. He handled it as though it were a sacred object. The map was also greeted with enthusiasm. Especially the part marked Outside.

"Outside? Is it true?" asked Vocata, as his fingers traced the path from his Reach town to the world he had only heard tell of in legend.

"It is where I have been living these past several days," I offered.

"My father never told me about Outside," he wistfully replied. Clearly overwhelmed, he sat in silence for a moment, and then asked, "Did the slowlis give you anything else?"

Not thinking it of great consequence, I had all but forgotten the small coin in my bag. When I produced this minor object, Vocata turned pale and trembled. Then, reaching inside of his shirt, he revealed an identical coin hung around his neck on a leather thong. He left his seat and embraced me. I was a little taken aback, but I stood and returned the old man's hug. Though it felt strange to be held by Vocata, it also seemed vaguely familiar. He held me for a long time, wetting my shoulders with his tears, as his decrepit body was racked by sobs.

Finally pulling away from me, he managed to ask, "Is this but a glorious dream I am experiencing?"

Tears started in my eyes then too. I didn't know why. "Dreams don't feel this real," I finally muttered, as I held his arm to steady him.

* * *

We all thought it might be wise for me to hide out for a while, until it appeared that Gamious gave up the chase for me. The plan was for me to take supplies and stay for a time in the caverns of the Otherworlder; the same I had made my entrance to Innerland through two months previously. Vocata was to gather as many Ancients as were still loyal to the principles the Deliverer taught, and meet me there to discuss what to do about Gamious in one week's time.

Before leaving to gather the Ancients that morning, Vocata gave me a leather thong to hang my metal coin around my neck. The thong, like the coin, resembled what he wore. I was honored by his gift, and thanked him reverently.

After Miyab changed the dressings on my foot wound, I prepared to leave. She was as good a physician as she was a cook. The continued pain was more bearable as she put a pinkish salve over the exposed layers of skin. She gave me a generous supply of the ointment, along with plenty of provisions from her pantry. I would certainly eat well during my voluntary internment.

Tabob had returned, and volunteered to go with me to the caverns. He proudly sported the shirt I had screened for him. I think he thought I had done a pretty good job getting away from the guards, even if I did run the wrong direction. As I said farewell to Vocata and Miyab, Mib stood a little off in the distance. Pounce was resting comfortably on her shoulder, black hair cascading like a waterfall across the back of the green tree-climber. Out of all of my surrogate family, it was hardest to say goodbye to her. I had stirrings of feelings for Mib that I couldn't quite explain. I didn't want to be away from her, not even for another week. As she approached me, I could tell that she shared those feelings.

"I will miss you, Jeff, "she finally uttered. "I feel I will not be seeing you for a long time."

"Only about a week, your father said," I reassured her.

"I know that's what he said, but..." she broke off gradually as a tear slowly drained from her left eye. After composing herself, she continued, "Take Pounce with you. He's missed you terribly, and I don't want you to be alone." I realized that this was a difficult sacrifice for her, knowing she loved the little green rodent as much as I did. Without a sound, Pounce jumped over to my shoulder and settled himself into the cowls of my cloak. I reached down and hugged my friend Mib, then departed.

"See you soon, " I said as cheerfully as I could muster. She smiled bravely in reply.

Tabob and I made it seemingly undetected to the Great Door. It had been ages since I had last been here. Everything so far seemed to be going according to plan. But then Tabob started abruptly when he attempted to open the secret panel to release the door.

"What's the matter?" I whispered as he cautiously stepped back. Pounce had become alert, and was sniffing the air wildly.

"Someone has tampered with the door recently. See?" Tabob showed me the inside mechanism of the door. I didn't see, but I nodded my head anyway, supposing that he knew what he was talking about. "Let's proceed carefully," he offered, as we slipped through the giant doorway.

Together, Tabob and I walked for a while longer, until we finally negotiated the second, smaller door. It was the same door that I had first come through that day long ago when I first met Tabob. Funny, it didn't seem to take as long to walk the distance from West Reach this last time, as it did to get there that first day. But then, I had done a lot of walking during the past few months also. We leisurely set our bedrolls and provisions in the living compartments that had been chiseled out anciently. Tired or not, it felt good to rest and get off of my foot, which was by this time beginning to ache more intensely. Our reverie was suddenly broken by a shout!

"Death to traitors against the Great Center Judge!" Curly shouted as he shot an arrow at my head. I ducked, just in time to avoid being hit! He somehow didn't seem as funny to me as he had at our first two meetings.

"Come!" screamed Tabob, as he grabbed my hand and pulled me after him. I had barely a fraction of a second to grab my sword and satchel. Pounce held on pretty well by himself. His tree-climbing claws would likely come in handy as we jostled and shifted on our way.

We ran aimlessly down several tunnels. I was not as out of breath this time as during my first trek. I also didn't stop to think about where we might be going. My single thought, as Tabob dragged me after him, was survival. I knew that the host of soldiers that followed plotted our destruction. After running for about fifteen to twenty minutes without a rest, I could tell that Tabob and I were both starting to tire. My right foot was on fire with pain.

Rounding a turn, we came suddenly upon a dead-end. Looking up, we found an opening in the ceiling above us. Tabob again commanded that I should follow him. I didn't argue as a second arrow whistled past my shoulder. We stumbled and fell into the darker tunnels a level or two up. The area we had come to seemed vaguely familiar. My foot hurt. I didn't have much time to think much about either, as more arrows (coming closer to their marks now) began to signal the arrival of our pursuers.

Tabob ran on in the lead towards a lighter tunnel. The guards of Gamious were close behind. A few let off some wild shots that missed us, but encouraged us to keep on at our break-neck pace. Running lengthwise across the sloping surface of this tunnel reminded me of running down the inside of an oil drum. Boy, how my foot screamed for a rest!

Suddenly Tabob called out. When I turned around, into the light, Tabob was no longer in front of me. As my momentum from running carried me into a tumbling free-fall over the edge of a bottomless cliff, I recognized momentarily the gigantic, inert form of my father that I had not seen in months. Frantically clutching at empty air, it suddenly occurred to me why the tunnel had seemed so familiar.

-CHAPTER FOURTEEN-
Judgment Day, Revisited

"...reality. This is not just a fantasy world!" yelled my dad, "No one is waiting for you to rescue them. But your teacher is waiting for you to finish your homework. Now get busy!"

I looked at my dad in astonishment. I was no longer falling through empty space, but was seated at my study desk in my bedroom. The room and surroundings must have been familiar to me at one time. Yet, at this moment, my new environment was as foreign to me as anything I had experienced during the last couple of months. I stared at my dad in dumb silence for a long moment. Then, not knowing what else to do (and probably due to the shock of being back) I put my head in my hands, and started to weep.

"Jeff? Jeff, what's the matter?" Dad looked at me, and then bent towards me with a concern I had never felt from him before, and gave me a friendly hug. I didn't know exactly why I was back in my world, but it felt good to be held by my father, even for just that short moment.

Pausing in our embrace, Dad backed away, an expression of puzzlement twisting his features. Then he really looked at me. "Jeff? What happened to your shoes? And your... pants?" he asked suspiciously as he finally noticed the kilt I wore. He thoughtfully tilted his head, as if the clothing I wore stirred up some deep forgotten memory. He had to have noticed the bleeding of my right foot next, because suddenly he became ashen faced, and exclaimed, "Oh my word!" Dashing out the door, he headed downstairs; hopefully to the bathroom for some first aid. By this time my foot was giving me the sharpest pain I had yet felt. My race to escape the guards had almost worn away the bandage Miyab had wrapped my foot with earlier that morning.

The short while Dad was gone I was left to ponder the situation. How could I be running from Gamious' thugs one moment, and then come back within a split second of the conversation I last remember having with my father? I had been gone for at least two months!

What was that Iamb had said? Oh yeah. Something about the time of our two world's being discrepant, not matching each other concisely. Perhaps the entire period I spent among the Inlanders had been compressed into a space of time that from our reckoning occupied less than our smallest instant. Then, for a fleeting moment anyhow, it all sort of made sense.

But feeling that I understood why didn't make me feel any better. I once thought, while back in Innerland, that I would eventually have to return to my world. I didn't want the time to be here yet. I realized that I had to get back there. Now!

The slowlis had also mentioned that the last Deliverer thought he had left only for overnight. Then when he returned (in what he thought was the next morning) eight cycles had passed in Innerland. If a couple of Inland months had passed in one of our seconds, how many cycles might be passing in the long minutes I had been sitting here in a stymie?

Most of the Inlanders were blind to Gamious' treachery, or intimidated by his faulty logic. The Reaches had not yet been made aware of his plans to enslave them. They needed a Deliverer, just as Iamb had told me. If for nothing else, the people needed someone to warn them. I had overheard his plans. I had to be the one to shout the warning. There was no time to worry about why fate had chosen me to fill that role. Quite simply, if I continued to wonder about my course of action without acting, hundreds of thousands of Inlanders could perish in the mines, if they hadn't been enslaved already.

OK. Calm down, Jeff, I thought, not feeling very calm. *Think.* Iamb theorized that the way I had been able to enter their world without the Stone of Recognition in the first place had to do with my imagination. My own creativity, coupled with the great emotion I had experienced during my heated argument with Dad, had worked the transfer. I never found the Stone of Recognition that previous Deliverers had used to move between worlds, not during any of the adventures I had experienced in Innerland. Even so, perhaps imagination and emotion could cause the transfer without needing the Stone again. I had to try. I attempted to concentrate on the anger I had felt at my father for destroying my comic collection. I tried to recall the details. *Concentrate. Concentrate! CONCENTRATE!!* Try as I might, it did not work for me now as it had then. That argument happened months ago (or was it seconds?) when my greatest challenge was whether or not to do my homework for school. All that seemed so trivial! The feelings I had then weren't enough to get my emotions to a state in which I could make the transition now.

Dad returned with the first aid kit and began to clean my injury. I tried to hate him, as I thought I had during that argument so long ago. I tried, I really did. But all that I could feel for him was the love a son sometimes feels for his dad. I realized that I had missed him. Even though I hadn't thought about him for a long time, I missed him. He hadn't spoken or looked at me since he had returned with the kit and started working on my foot. Even so, for that moment before he left, he had hugged me. He had been concerned. Concerned for me. I had not felt these feelings for my dad since Mom had died. Feelings of affection that I'd felt for him before Mom's death began all of a sudden to rise to the surface. Past the hatred I had felt for his not giving her a funeral. Past the countless arguments and differences we had experienced during the past few years. While he silently continued to clean and bandage my wound, I had the urge to hug my father back.

But before I could reach my arms out to embrace him, we were suddenly made aware of another person in the room. A low groan of complaint came from the far side of my bed. *Tabob!* In the shock of being back I had forgotten all about him. Dad screamed for me to take cover, and ran next door to his room. What is Dad doing now? I thought in confusion. I wasn't left to wonder long as Dad quickly returned brandishing a pistol!

"No, Dad! Tabob's my friend!" I screamed as I stood up, suddenly wincing with pain as I stood on my damaged foot. Tabob stood erect now, rubbing his head and looking around, wearing a rather perplexed look. If the muscle-bound teenager had looked like a giant in Innerland, he looked more a colossus as he dwarfed the new surroundings of my room. Any self-respecting body-builder would have been jealous! At the mention of the name Tabob, Dad had begun to lower his revolver. Before we were able to make formal introductions, however, we were interrupted yet another time. An arrow zipped past my waist, narrowly missing me and imbedding itself in my dad's right hand.

Three things then happened simultaneously. Dad dropped his gun, which fired off a wild shot that hit the wall. The guard I had nicknamed Curly, appeared and crashed into my desk, knocking it and me into a heap on the ground with him. Tabob screamed a battle cry, and leaped across my bed towards us.

"West Reach!" screamed my giant friend, as he unsheathed his sword, in preparation to attack Curly.

Ker-Lee quickly readied his own sword, and deflected Tabob's downward thrust while pushing me to the side, out of his way. I'd have kicked him if my foot hadn't hurt so badly! Tabob and Ker-Lee parried one another's blows for long moments. The melee looked like a scene from a good action movie, and probably would have been exciting to watch, if it had not been for the knowledge that these two men were in a death struggle. Tabob fell to the ground, slipping on a sheet from my unmade bed. Ker-Lee raised his sword for the kill.

By that time, my dad had broken the arrow and removed it from his hand. Ignoring his bleeding palm, he reached over and pulled the wooden sheath sword from where it was strapped on my back: I had forgotten that it was there! Leaping over my prostrate form, Dad brought the sword (still in it's scabbard) down firmly across the back of Curly's skull. There was a loud cracking sound. Ker-Lee stood there tottering for a moment. Then, as his eyes glazed over, he dropped his weapon, and fell face first onto my bed.

"Way to go Dad!" I congratulated as I jumped over and hugged him. I ignored the sharp pain as I stood again, my emotions feeling stronger just then than my physical discomfort. Dad just smiled back at me, relief showing in his face as he reached over and tousled my hair.

Subtle claws on my shoulder, accompanied by a small whimper, signaled the return of Pounce. He must have made the transition too, and had been hiding during the confusion. I didn't stop to think it funny at the time, that rather than acting surprised, Dad reached over and scratched my pet rodent's head, saying, "Hi there, little glib. Decided it's safe to join the party now?"

Tabob deftly bound Ker-Lee's hands and feet with a length of rope he produced from his satchel. A groaning sigh of complaint indicated that Gamious' guard was still alive. Tabob turned to my dad and extended his arm in friendship. "My thanks for your timely intervention, fellow warrior! I am Tabob Guard. What is the name you are called by?"

Taking his outstretched hand, my dad smiled and replied, "Thomas. Thomas Ransford." Tabob looked at my dad in stunned silence. Then, after briefly examining the pattern on the hem of

Tabob's kilt, Dad added, "It is good to meet you, third-son of Vocata," causing me to numbly look at my dad as well.

Still in a daze, Tabob dropped his weapon, grabbed my dad's outstretched hand with both of his, and knelt in obeisance to him! Tabob was kneeling before my dad! *Tabob was kneeling before my dad?*

"Grandfather..." Tabob whispered, "Great Deliverer."

The many turns of events during the last several minutes had my head spinning. This last event caused me to stop and see things I had not before realized. Many things I had heard during the last two months suddenly came into focus: Vocata knowing my name, and having me wear the family colors. Iamb teaching me almost exclusively about the history of the last Deliverer, and then reacting with sadness when I asked what that Deliverer's name had been. Even back to not having a funeral for my mom after Dad had said she'd been killed during a business trip. My mom was the woman who had to return to Innerland in order to survive. She was also the wife that had been left behind in her world. Her baby born there, Vocata, was my brother. The last Deliverer was... *my dad!*

* * *

Curly spent the afternoon tied up in the washroom, while Dad, Tabob and I visited the emergency room and the fast-food joint. Pounce also stayed, nestled into the comforter on my unmade bed. As Dad drove around, I secretly hoped that Tabob had been able to tie better knots than the palace guards had done; it would not be good to let a warrior like Ker-Lee loose in my world.

Dad insisted Tabob and I both change clothes before we made our rounds. I was in my own realm again, and felt comfortable in my old duds. But Tabob looked miserable. The loose fitting Levis he had borrowed from Dad weren't loose, and the Mickey Mouse tee shirt was like a second layer of skin. Even so, Tabob could almost pass as someone from my world in the clothes Dad had loaned him, that is, if no one looked too closely.

The doctor on duty at the emergency room (Dr. Derma) was able to alleviate the pain I was feeling from my second run-in with the gum-paste. She washed my wound with an antibiotic soap, and covered the bottom of my foot with an ointment that relieved it even more than Miyab's home remedies had. She kept having to ask Tabob, who looked on in fascination as she worked, to stand back. The really great thing was the artificial skin-sock she gave me to wear. She called it telfa-moleskin; it was a thing usually used for burn victims.

Anyway, it made my foot feel almost normal to walk around on. Even so, she warned me not to walk around too much on my foot until it healed or it would again become unbearable. When she asked me how I had lost the skin I told her I had been playing around with super-glue. My dad hid his face in his hands to keep from laughing when Tabob corrected me and pointed out that it was gum-paste. I don't think the doctor believed either of us.

Our visit to a fast-food restaurant on the way home went well. It was sure good to taste a hamburger again. I didn't note exactly how many burgers Tabob downed; I lost count. Suffice it to say, my dad spent a lot more on dinner than he had counted on. Dad was pretty nice to Tabob though, and even bought him a collector cup. Tabob thought the featured basketball player looked like 'a great warrior.'

During the dinner we talked briefly. Dad wouldn't tell me anything about his being a Deliverer. He kept saying something about it being against an ancient code to tell another Deliverer until they had first figured out their own purpose. Since I hadn't yet figured out mine, he couldn't tell me much. That just got me frustrated, because by then I was more curious than ever. It was as aggravating as talking with Iamb!

"Jeff, I don't understand this whole thing yet, even having lived within Innerland myself. But I know it is for your benefit that you need to be the one to find out. Anything more that I might say about it might foul up what is destined to be," he explained.

"Yeah. But I'd still like to know," I persisted.

"I know, Son, and you will. But this is something you'll have to trust yourself on."

The drive home was uneventful. Ker-Lee was still tied up when we arrived, and had fallen asleep. I'm glad Tabob could tie a good knot. Our captive would not take any food from us when we woke him up to offer, so we left him alone. Dad said he would guard him during the night. He then sent Tabob and I up to my room to get some sleep.

I thought over what my dad had said, about 'trusting myself.' Exhausted as I felt, I still didn't sleep much that night for wondering about my purpose.

Looking around, I saw that Dad had replaced my comics on the shelf by my desk. I think he saw it as a token of apology for knocking them off earlier. It was a nice gesture, but he needn't have bothered. The adventure I had always hoped for, my venture into Innerland, had so far been nothing like the stories in the comics I read about. Comics. I never thought that I would ever think them moronic. I was realizing that people, and the lives they lived, were not as shallow as the two-dimensional characters I read about in my comics. Decisions were also not always that black and white.

Wandering around my disheveled room, my eye fell on the one comic not on my shelf. It was the copy of Captain Amazing I had been reading the night before. To me it had been two months of nights before. I opened it, and read.

He knew even as his ship came into orbit around the planet that nothing could stop him from his appointed mission. Nothing could distract him from fulfilling the destiny he was meant for. These people depended on him. "I am to be their deliverer!" he said aloud, with a feeling of excitement. "They are counting on me to..."

I crumpled up the comic and made a perfect basket into the wastecan beside my desk.

"Why'd you do that?" asked Tabob as he retrieved the comic. After looking at it for a few minutes, he exclaimed, "Hey! This guy looks like me!" I didn't have the heart to tell him that the drawing on his own shirt was Captain A, with Tabob's head drawn on.

Shutting off my light, and plopping down on my unmade bed, I pulled the blankets over my head and prepared for sleep. Somehow, I had to get back to Innerland. No matter how much time had passed, it was my destiny to be the Deliverer for Vocata (my newfound brother) and his people. I was to be a Deliverer, as my father, and his father before him had been.

-CHAPTER FIFTEEN-
The Stone of Recognition

Tabob must have been as excited as I was about recent events. He had gotten to meet the former Deliverer; his grandfather. I had discovered that I'd lived with the Deliverer all of my life. He was none other than my father! Tabob kept asking questions until I thought I'd never fall asleep. *Had I been that much of a bother with my questions in his world?* I hoped not.

I was exhausted when I finally fell asleep, with Pounce curled around the top of my head. As I began to make the transition from this world into dream-land, I realized that I had better rest well; a lot was riding on what we could figure out the next day, and I wanted to be as fresh as I could for it. It has always been easier for me to face a problem when I'm fresh, first thing in the morning. I welcomed my eventual slip into the warm darkness of slumber. Just as I was almost out, I was interrupted again. The disturbance came not from Tabob, but from another familiar voice.

Jeff.

"Leave me alone, Mib," I replied sleepily

Jeff.

"C'mon, I'm serious. Your brother has kept me up all night... I need some sleep!" I was beginning to feel a bit testy.

Jeff.

I sat up in bed, tired to the point of anger. "Mib, you're my best friend and all, but..." My words trailed off into nothingness. I was not in the familiar surroundings of my room. Pounce was nowhere to be seen. I was not on Earth, yet I knew I was not in Innerland either. I sat on a rectangular vault in a sort of stone tomb (like the ones I'd seen in old issues of National Geographic.) It was not dark, for the many candles, torches, and glow bones arranged around the room. Glow bones. So I must be back. The room I was in looked more like a chamber in Outside than the homes in Innerland. However, it didn't have the authentic feel that I had sensed residing in that world over the last few months. This time it was a dream. I was aware of my dreaming, and knew I was not really there. I longed to be back, but realized that the sooner I slept, the sooner I'd awake. I lay back down on my side and closed my eyes.

Suddenly I felt a warm touch on my shoulder. I sat bolt upright! *Jeff.*

The same voice that had called me from sleep before... I had thought it was Mib, but now, being a little more aware, I realized that it would not be Mib's face that I would see when I turned around. Standing slender and tall before me was the most beautiful woman I had ever before laid eyes on, awake or dreaming. She wore the garb of an Inlander, except that her dress was a brilliant white and shimmered. Her hair was waist-length, and black. Each feature of her face and body were more perfect than even a Hollywood model could have been made to look. As she held a hand towards me to beckon me, I noticed that the hem on her garment boasted the same patterns as the designs on Vocata's house.

Jeff. I realized for the first time that the melodic voice was in my mind, that she did not move her lips when speaking. It was just as Iamb had done.

I seemed lost in her beauty and hypnotic voice. "Who are you?" I finally managed.

Jeff. Has it been so long, my little warrior? She responded, as her perfect lips slowly formed into a kindly smile.

Little warrior? I had not heard that since... "Mother!" I exclaimed as I rushed forward and embraced that perfect being. "Mom," I muttered as she enfolded me in her embrace. As my sobs came more freely, I began to realize how bitterly I had missed her these past few years.

We stood there hugging for a long time. I gave vent to every emotion. Finally, I pulled away from her embrace, gazed into her eyes, and began to ask, "How-?" but was cut off as she put her index finger gently to my lips.

We've no time for lengthy explanations just now, she counseled. *But we do have a little time to talk. And I have some things to show you, Deliverer,* she added.

We sauntered down lengthy corridors, each successive one as well lit as the one that preceded it. She held my hand and commented on how proud she was of me, and of my efforts to improve my drawings. I thought it was great that she thought my interests were of importance. She also commented on how brave she thought I had been in facing the challenges I had in Innerland. My mom's praise for me did a lot for my esteem. I knew it was just a dream, but dream or not, it sure felt good talking to Mom again. I had forgotten how much I had missed the conversations we had together.

Rounding a corner, we came to a familiar room: the antechamber that Iamb had given me the former Deliverer's (my father's) treasures in! We approached the dais in the center of the room. As I turned towards Mom, she simply flashed me a knowing smile. Turning back to the waist-high table, she made a sweeping motion with her hand, after which the stone slab noiselessly slid to the side, leaving the vault open. Mom reached inside and removed a small object, which she then handed to me. I looked at the familiar brown leather book, complete with brass hinges and hasp that she placed in my hands. Then came an immediate rush of excitement: she had just given me my father's journal!

Jeff, she spoke to my thoughts, as she sat on the edge of the vault, inviting me to do likewise, *I give you three gifts. These gifts are yours to use to discover how you might deliver the people of Innerland, some of which you now know are kin. As Iamb taught, in order for you to have true power, you must discover your destiny and work for yourself. Nevertheless, I give you these three gifts to enable you to attain your potential as Deliverer, and to help you discover your true purpose. Remember, Son: life without purpose is worse than not living.*

The first gift I give to you is the gift of experience. Due to the interruption of the process of your gaining experience among my people by Gamious, you stayed shorter among the Inlanders than you should have. So I now right that wrong by giving you the experience of your father. I knew that she referred to the journal my father kept as he journeyed and lived among these people. As much as I was enjoying this visit with Mom, I could hardly wait to read my father's history.

She then continued. *The second gift I give you, Son, is the gift of strength beyond your cycles.* She reached forward and firmly squeezed the muscle of my right arm. *Let me into your thoughts for a moment as you think back upon your experiences with Gamious, and you will understand.* As I relaxed, my thoughts came quickly upon several instances. I recalled the rock embedded in Gamious' carriage, the one I had thrown from a distance. I remembered the ease with which I loosened the ropes on two different occasions. I thought upon my crazy multi-staged leap across the gum paste. And

I thought upon my ability to wrench my foot free from the gum paste without assistance. Then, it occurred to me what the gift was which my mother now gave to me. It had really been there all along, yet I had not known it until now.

"I am somehow stronger here, than on Earth, aren't I," I stated more than asked.

Mom nodded her head. *Iamb referred superficially to the time differential. There are other discrepancies between our worlds. Another difference somehow involves the pull of gravity having less of an affect on Otherworlders here than on Inlanders. This is why my son, Vocata, and each in his family, are more robust than the typical Inlander. As with the other gifts I have given you to use in our world, use this gift carefully, Jeff.*

"Speaking of 'worlds,' just where is Innerland, Mom?"

You have already discovered the answer for that question for yourself, my son, though you have not yet accepted it. And this brings us to the third, and final gift—that of wisdom. She gently touched the temples of my head with the fore- and middle fingers of each hand, and then continued. *Just as you knew you could place trust in your younger brother Vocata, and as you likewise wisely knew to distrust Gamious and your nephew Corun, trust your inner-feelings. There is dormant wisdom there that is not yet been awakened. Trust yourself, and those who you feel impressed you can confide in. If you are true to yourself, you will never go wrong.*

She then embraced me, and said softly, *Remember these gifts, my first-son. Remember too that I love and miss you. I must go now, but we will meet again at the end of your journeys.* We hugged tightly again. I did not want to leave, but knew I must let her go. After a blissful eternity of embrace, we stood.

Holding my shoulders, she spoke her final words, *Stay here for as long as you like. Read your father's words. When you have finished, retrace your steps to the place you first met me tonight. Lay on my crypt in slumber, and you will thereafter awaken in your world again. I must go now, First-Son. Do well in your life, and know that I love you, now and always.*

I told her that I loved her too. We hugged again, and then she walked slowly away. I eventually was able to control my deep emotions somewhat and turned back to my father's book. Despite my tears, I soon became absorbed in my father's history. I read for what seemed hours, and I grew fatigued before I grew close to finishing my father's record. Growing too tired to continue reading, I closed the journal, and retraced my steps down the brightly lit corridors to what my mother had identified as her tomb. Gathering my father's journal to my bosom, I fell into a deep and profound, dreamless sleep; more restful than any I before remember.

* * *

I slowly woke amid the familiar surroundings of my old room. The bed was not as comfortable as the one I had begun to grow used to in Vocata's house. Pounce was still sleeping peacefully and warm, wrapped around my head. I rolled over onto something hard, which poked me in my side: my father's journal! At breakfast, I showed it to him.

He smiled, handed the journal back to me, and gave me a knowing look that precluded my explaining the dream-visit with Mom. He then said, "I'm glad you can have that, Jeff. It is too bad that the code of Deliverers precluded me telling you about those experiences before you found Innerland on your own. That is the safeguard put down by the first Deliverer in antiquity. My father never told me about his experiences before I had my journeys either. There will be time to talk later, Son."

Tabob was funny about the breakfast cereal. I laughed when he asked who the ruler was pictured on the front of a King Munchies cereal box. Even though he was disappointed that the fellow pictured was not really a king, he must have enjoyed the cereal because he consumed five mixing bowls full of it! Dad noticed the look on my face when I realized Tabob had eaten all of my favorite cereal, and then assured me he would purchase more that afternoon. Pounce preferred just plain corn flakes. He sat on the table alongside me as we ate and talked.

"What about the Stone of Recognition, Dad?" I queried. "I think it would make our transition back to Innerland easier, and more sure, from what Iamb taught me."

"Certainly," agreed my father. "But remember what that overgrown lizard also must have taught you."

I gave my dad a puzzled look. He continued.

"You have to discover the pieces for yourself, in order for the power to work. You have great power already son, to have made a transition to Innerland and back without the Stone in the first place. Think on what you know already, and you will discover the Stone for yourself."

I thought hard, all during breakfast, but this answer did not come as easily as others had with Mom's help last night.

After allowing Ker-Lee to eat and stretch a bit we re-tied him up, and began to pack various items for our journey. Every time I bent over, the coin that hung around my neck kept falling out and getting in my way. It became almost a habit to sling the thing out of the way. I wasn't used to wearing a necklace, and I wondered why Vocata had encouraged me to wear it.

I wasn't sure I agreed that we would need all of the stuff Dad suggested we take. I remembered how tired I had gotten walking with nothing on my back, and these packs were quickly becoming heavy!

"But why would I need a tape recorder, Dad?" I asked, becoming annoyed.

"Why do you think I had such a reputation for appropriate judgment? I had tape recorders installed in the preparation chambers before both parties presented their cases."

I looked at Dad for a moment, dumfounded. "You cheated!" I finally asserted. Tabob looked like he was going to clobber me for talking to my dad that way.

Dad just smiled, and then continued, "Maybe... at first anyway. I really did get to the point that I could pretty well tell who was lying and who would be truthful. You might find it useful though, and since it doesn't weigh much, take it along." He stuffed it in the side of my pack, and I kind of forgot that it was there. He also stuffed the pack with a set of walkie-talkies, as well as various other items, in addition to food and our normal backpacking provisions. I thought that since we were taking all the other hi-tech stuff that Dad might loan me his revolver. He declined; however, saying he didn't think it was a good idea.

The coin hanging on a leather tong around my neck fell in front of me again, fouling my hands for about the thousandth time. Annoyed, I was about to take it off and put it in my pocket so that it would stop bothering me. As I held it in my hand, I remembered that I hadn't asked Dad why he had bothered to put this object in with the other artifacts Iamb had shown me. I figured he wouldn't tell me, but I attempted to ask him anyway.

"Why did you put this in the antechamber for me to find, Dad?" I asked as I held it up. "I remember seeing some other coins like them when I was younger, but I don't quite remember where." Dad smiled mischievously, and quite suddenly I did remember where I had seen a coin like this before: playing with Dad's coin collection as a young boy!

Hanging the coin back around my neck, I let out a whoop as I bolted next door to my Dad's room. I even remembered which desk drawer he kept the box of coins in, though it had been years since I had played with them as a small child. Dad looked on approvingly as I sat the cigar-box on his ink blotter.

Opening the box, and sifting through its contents, I remembered why the collection had held so much magic for me as a small boy. I had always referred to it as Dad's 'coin collection', but I now recalled that it contained other treasures in addition the vast assortment of oddly shaped coins from other countries. There was a spindle of lava from a volcano, not even as big around as my pinky, a tin dime-store compass, various sea-stones, broaches, pins, tie tacks and a menagerie of other treasures- A pile of expensive looking (but probably worthless) stuff. Then I saw it. I had never paid any special attention to that stone before, yet now I knew it for what it was, as if I had always known it: *the Stone of Recognition!*

The Stone was jet black, except for a thick fissure of ivory with a few branches that cut its surface. The white portions of the Stone were pocked with great age. Overall, it looked as though it had been weathered for millennia on the shore of the sea. Its pattern was irregular, but roughly teardrop in shape. Attached to the Stone was a lengthy chain, interrupted by tiny metal plates the length of my fingernail, and about a quarter its width. I counted fourteen links between each connecting plate. The black of the Stone deepened in intensity from the oil in my hands as I touched it and rolled it in my fingers. How it looked physically did not compare with what I knew it could do, or rather, what I could do with it. It was ironic that I had ignorantly played with this thing of power as a child.

"Well done, First-Son," my father congratulated, as he gently laid a hand upon my shoulder. "You are now nearly ready to depart." I carefully placed the Stone on the chain around my neck. I now had my passport to Innerland. I was ready to go! *Or was I?* Nagging doubts and fears began to unsettle my resolve.

"Will you go with us, Dad?" I asked, feeling suddenly unsure of myself.

He simply smiled, and shook his head. "No," he replied, after a few long moments. "My time and influence in Innerland are ended. It is now for you to use your time and influence to bring about a good which you will soon discover." He put his hand around my shoulder as we left his office. I felt strengthened by his firm touch.

When we re-entered my bedroom, Ker-Lee looked up from his seated position on the chair, saw the necklace and the Stone dangling around my neck, and then pitched forward onto his knees. Pounce yawned, saw me, and leapt to my shoulder, purring contentedly.

Ker-Lee remained on his knees in a prostrate position. "Forgive me, Deliverer," he wept.

I looked confusedly at Dad. He removed his hand from my shoulder, and nodded for me to approach the man.

Pretending greater authority than I felt, I asked him, "Do you now know me for who I am?"

He nodded yes. Then I got bolder.

"Will you denounce your allegiance to the tyrant Gamious, and follow me in my quest?"

He softly replied, "Yes."

I reached over and cut his bonds. I now knew I could trust him. Tabob looked shocked though, and remained on his guard.

"Ker-Lee is our brother now," I said to reassure Tabob. "Get him to help us pack."

Tabob obliged. It felt good to have Dad's approval, as I looked his direction and caught his smile and the subtle nodding of his head. I believed in the gift of wisdom Mom had given me. It had now shown me an ally in he who I thought to be an enemy.

Dad said goodbye, wished me good fortune, and then stepped out of the room. Closing my eyes, and holding the Stone of Recognition in my right hand, I pictured in my mind the living cubicles that Tabob and I were supposed to have waited in for Vocata's return with the Elders of Innerland. A slight tingling sensation passed throughout my entire body, accompanied by a faint breeze on my face and hands. Pounce growled in apprehension. When I opened my eyes a moment later, the three of us (with Pounce and our packs) stood just on the other side of the first small, carved door. It was exactly the place I had pictured in my mind as we had stood in my bedroom. Boy! The transition was certainly managed a lot easier with the Stone, than it had been my first trip into Innerland.

    I didn't have time to reflect of the comfort of the transition between Earth and Innerland however, as our reflections were interrupted by the blood curdling scream of a woman on the other side of the door!

-CHAPTER SIXTEEN-
Time Moves on Without Me

My nephew Tabob, a new friend Ker-Lee, my pet glib Pounce, and I had just made a successful transition back into Innerland mere moments before. We stood inside the living compartments of the Otherworlders. I had thought we might first settle down and plan how we would go about contacting Vocata. Next I would attempt to discover why I was sent at this time as a Deliverer. My ultimate purpose in being here was still somewhat hidden from me. However, time was not a luxury that we were afforded at the particular moment. Hearing the scream of a woman galvanized our small alliance into action. We had no idea who had screamed, or what was the need. Yet that didn't matter: a fellow human was in trouble, and we were available to help. Almost as one our little band rushed through the doorway to assist the unknown victim.

Standing in the middle of the chamber before us, singlehandedly trying to fend off eight or ten men, was a single woman. She had black, shoulder length hair, like many of the women in Innerland. I couldn't see her face, but she did not seem old, probably a little younger than Tabob. In contrast to other women I had seen in this world, she wielded a sword, and seemed very skilled with it. A hastily discarded pack lay at her feet, and her shirt was torn. She fought, holding a blade in her right hand, while she attempted to maintain some degree of dignity with her left hand holding her tunic pulled loosely over her shoulder. The slob who had apparently torn her clothes lay unconscious (with a bloodied face) at her feet, alongside her discarded pack. The attitude of the other guards indicated that they meant to do her malevolent harm. The situation infuriated me! What added further to the rage beginning to seethe within me was the easily recognizable identity of her attackers: They were all Judge Guards!

The telfa skin covering which the doctor had put on my foot at the emergency room worked as well as she had said it would. It made the agonizing pain I had felt a day before seem now to be only a large discomfort. Compared to how my foot had slowed me on my escape yesterday, it didn't seem to even phase me now.

As our threesome vaulted through the door in unison, I launched my body into the nearest attacker. I had two brief hopes as my enemy turned to face me. First, I hoped that what Mom had told me about my being a bit stronger in Innerland was a true gift that I could count on at this time. Secondly, I hoped that the self-defense moves I had learned in gym class from coach Nakitani could be used as an effective offensive weapon.

Within my foe's range, I took his first punch to my mouth. It hurt like blazes and didn't sound at all like the punches on TV, or look as glamorous as the fights in my many comics. The impact was a sickening squash, which I felt reverberate through my entire body. My mouth stung badly and started to bleed. But I didn't fall down, which surprised my opponent and me. While he gazed at me in fascinated shock, Pounce jumped at his face, chattering and scratching at his unprotected features. The guard tried unsuccessfully to pull the screaming glib from his head. While Pounce had him occupied, I used the first move that came to mind: I launched an upward kick between his legs. You may not think that my kick was fair, but the guy was a lot bigger than me. Besides, I was fighting for my life! I chose the target more from reflex than maliciousness. Anyway, when the guy bent over in pain, Pounce jumped behind me and scurried for cover. I didn't blame the glib for not hanging around: the guard meant business, and I didn't want my pet hurt, or in the way. I also didn't want the guard to sneak up on me while I was busy with someone else, so while he was still doubled over, I leaned down and cold-cocked him. He slumped to the ground, unconscious.

As I stood, two guards on either side of me fluidly lowered their cocked crossbows in my direction, and fired! In a flash of insight, I remembered a situation like this in my comics. Almost instantly I dropped to the dusty cavern floor. I felt the air from the twin bolts as they simultaneously grazed my shoulders. As had happened in the comic, my adversaries impaled each other. Before I could congratulate myself on my ingenious defense, however, I witnessed the look of horror, eternally etched on the face of the man nearest me who had only moments before been a living, breathing human. Instead of smiling, I suddenly retched at the sight of his gruesome death.

As I wiped my mouth, a surprise blow to my ribs (by a burly fellow from behind me) knocked the wind from my lungs. As I crumpled over, gasping for air, my new foe mercilessly kicked me again and again with the heavy sole of his foot. I was about to pass out for lack of oxygen when surprisingly my attacker disappeared. I rolled over in time to see my assailant hefted physically off of his feet, and hurled across the cavern into a vertical wall. He was, of course, unconscious by the time he slid into a crumpled heap on the ground.

I caught my breath, and then looked back to discover the identity of my unknown benefactor. I discovered Ker-Lee helping me to my feet. After making certain I could stand on my own, he stepped between the melee and myself, allowing me an additional moment to finish catching my breath. My trust in him had proven well founded; as my mother claimed would be the case if I followed my inner feelings.

Ker-Lee then took a wide-legged stance, as if he were sitting on a horse. Squatting and raising his muscular arms heavenward made him look larger and even more formidable. Shouting with a resonant voice that momentarily stilled the confusion, Ker-Lee bellowed a challenge. "Hear me, dog guards of the slime king Gamious! I am Ker-Lee, just back from the dead. I now serve the Deliverer, and seek vengeance upon my renounced master. Face me, and you will die like him!"

Ker-Lee's impromptu oration, and the recent airborne body of their fallen comrade, was enough to break morale among the troops. Those still standing immediately broke rank and fled, accompanied by Ker-Lee's and Tabob's laughter. I slumped to the floor, delighted to be alive, and feverishly tried to figure out what we should do next. I glanced around to see where Pounce had hidden himself.

The girl we assisted turned, and rushed headlong into the surprised arms of Tabob. He looked at her as he pulled back, trying to make sense of her affectionate reaction. *Hey*, I thought, *Ker-Lee and I helped too!* Then, as her flowing black hair fell away revealing her face, I recognized my best friend in that teenage girl. Though several cycles older now, it was Mib!

"They told me that you had died cycles ago, older brother," Mib sobbed, through her tear streaked face. "I never believed it," she added. Tabob simply stared with his mouth half open, disbelief clouding his expression, as he looked her up and down.

She continued. "You and Jeff were gone for so long. Gamious claimed he'd had you both killed as traitors. He even outlawed the practice of a belief in a Deliverer among the Reaches. But I knew in my heart you were both still alive. I have come here every day for nearly eight cycles hoping to find you. I felt at each pilgrimage that you would return, alive. My meditations today have finally proven true."

"Mib... my little warrior," was all Tabob could manage, before he pulled her head to his bosom, holding her tight and tousling her full head of hair. I had never imagined Tabob capable of great emotion until I witnessed his tears coming freely that morning.

Eight cycles, I thought to myself. *Iamb told me the discrepancy between our exit and return would be eight cycles. She must be nearly sixteen cycles old now. I'm younger than she is!*

While brother and sister embraced, Ker-Lee tied the hands of the three that had been overcome by our small army. I continued to sit, my eyes intent upon my friend whom I had not seen since yesterday, and who had in turn not seen me for eight cycles. Mib jumped with surprise as a flying fur-ball wrapped itself around her shoulders.

So that's where he got himself to, I thought.

When Mib realized what (or who) the purring clump of green hair was, she looked around in excitement and asked, "Where is Jeff?"

I have not since felt as awkward as I did then. I knew it wasn't my fault, and it's kind of dumb when you think about it, yet I felt intimidated at suddenly being younger than her. I slowly stood, with a slight smirk of embarrassment, and said, not very eloquently, "Hi'ya Mib."

Her response was a little of a surprise to us all, and I didn't know quite how to take it. Was she glad to see me or not? I made it a point to ask her when she awoke from the fainting spell that had suddenly seized her.

* * *

A short time later, after Mib had overcome her shock and Ker-Lee had secured our prisoners, we all had a chance to rest for a bit and catch our breath. We decided not to stay long because we felt certain that additional guards would soon be deployed to our position. Ker-Lee splashed fluid from a water-skin over the faces of our three captives. "Get up, you scurvy dogs." The prisoners were sullen, especially the fellow I had kicked, but they complied with Ker-Lee's instructions. As we got the packs back in order, and prepared to leave, Mib hit us on the head with some disturbing information.

"Jeff. Tabob. There is a specific reason that I've come to the Great Door these past cycles. You remember that Father was to assemble the Ancients and bring them here to learn of Gamious' treachery?" Mib now had our full attention. "Gamious and his guards intercepted Father in his rounds eight cycles ago when you both left. Vocata has been a prisoner at the palace since that time."

"In the dungeons? No!" screamed Tabob as he unsheathed his sword in a fit of anger.

"No," replied Mib flatly, as she stepped forward and placed a restraining hand on her brother's arm. "At first he was simply kept from moving about Innerland in general. Mother visited him frequently, and finally decided to reside with him there about five cycles ago. For the last two and a half cycles his movements have been restricted solely to the palace. He is not any longer allowed visits from the other Ancients. I refused to move to the palace however, and have continued to live in West Reach, though it is not as you will remember it when you left."

"Gamious is too cowardly to have Father killed, but keeping him prisoner achieves the same ends," she continued. "Besides, recent changes in the government have made the Ancients powerless, except as traditional figureheads."

"We have to free him. That much is clear," I stated.

"How?" countered Tabob flatly, becoming more sensible now, since his initial outbreak of rage. "The palace is the best defense in Innerland. In ancient times the Reaches all warred among themselves. Power shifted often, yet the palace in Coreterior was never defeated. The former Deliverer himself designed and built it. He also directed his government from the Central Palace. I would have my father free as much as any of us. But that fortress is impregnable. What hope do our few have against that monstrosity, and the host that defend it?"

My instinct told me plainly that Vocata was a necessary part of whatever lay ahead. Not even the mightiest fortress in Innerland could stand between the three of us and getting him freed. "What you say about the fortress being strong may be true, my friend. However…" and with a flourish I held up my father's journal for all to see, then continued, "…I have the words of the last Deliverer, including sketches of the floor-plans of the Palace."

Smiles gradually came upon the faces of those present (except for the prisoners, of course) as they each in turn realized the implications of my revelation.

Ker-Lee, who up to that time had been silent, then stepped forward and spoke.

"The palace has never been defeated because none knew the defenses. Though we be a small band, we have the very plans for the Great Central Palace. There stands also one among you who has served many cycles at the palace, and is familiar with some subtle changes that have been made to defenses during the past several hundred cycles. I again offer you my loyal services, Deliverer," he said simply, as he bent to one knee before me.

I could have kissed him on his pudgy, bald, head! Instead, I smiled, helped him to his feet, and said, "C'mon Curly. We'll get back to West Reach and plan our attack there."

As we walked off, trailing three disgruntled prisoners in our wake, I felt fairly positive about our situation. We had survived our first ordeal fairly well, and had in fact beaten a foe that had outnumbered us. We possessed the combined plans and experience that should get us into the palace. With some planning and good fortune, we should manage to get out again with Vocata and Miyab as additions to our party. I could not see into the future, but I felt we had adequate reason to be optimistic.

Tabob and Ker-Lee walked ahead a ways to scout our path, towing the prisoners in their wake. Mib and I (and Pounce) brought up the rear. I still felt somewhat uncomfortable around the older version if Mib. We had not really spoken yet, and she was avoiding my gaze. How would you feel if your best friend was suddenly much older than you? She didn't much look like the girls my age either. She was becoming an enchantingly beautiful woman. I guess my still being a young boy physically was what bothered me most.

After a few awkwardly silent moments, Mib sauntered a little closer in my direction. She looked me over, smiled, and said candidly, "You really are a little boy!"

I frowned, and turned my head the other way.

"I'm sorry Jeff," Mib recanted. "I know you were sensitive about that before. A few cycles after you and Tabob left Father told me about your being from Otherworld. He mentioned that the passage of time was different and all. But this... this is a surprise!"

"It's a surprise for me too," I hissed. "When I saw you yesterday, you were an eight cycle old girl. At least from my perspective." Then, attempting to calm down a bit, I added, "It's hard for you too, isn't it?"

Mib nodded her head affirmatively as she continued to gaze at me. "I thought, when you and Tabob left eight cycles ago, that it might be a long time before I saw either of you again. But I never guessed that you and my brother would not age!"

"I'm still Jeff," I maintained.

"And I'm still Mib," she countered with a growing smile. After pausing for a moment, she reluctantly yet reverently asked, "Jeff? Are you... are you our Deliverer?"

I shrugged, and then replied, "Yes. Maybe. I have the Stone of Recognition now anyway," I said as I pulled the ebony pebble from my knapsack and dangled it in front of her mesmerized gaze.

She stopped walking, and knelt before me.

"Get up, Mib!" I demanded, in an embarrassed tone. "No matter what else I'm supposed to be, I'm still Jeff."

Walking beside me again, she changed the subject, "I wish you had aged, Jeff. I used to have a crush on you. I thought you were one of the handsomest men I had ever met."

I enjoyed spending time with Mib during my first visit to Innerland. Though it was brief, I believed we had become good friends. Lifetime friends, even. However, her newly revealed feelings surprised me!

She continued, "You looked a lot older to me then. Yet walking again with you now, even knowing I'm a few cycles older, I still feel like the little girl I was cycles ago, admiring the same handsome fellow," she said as she reached down and gently took my hand in hers. "I know a man like you could protect me from-"

"Mib!" I quickly interrupted before she could continue, "The Stone of Recognition..."

"Yes... Jeff..." she nodded, staring at me dreamy-eyed.

"It was given to me by the last Deliverer. My father," I blurted out, feeling quite agitated by her affectionate revelations. "He is Vocata's father also. Vocata, your father, is my brother." I waited for a few seconds, to allow time for the information to sink in.

"Then I... I... I'm your niece?" she stammered, as she quickly withdrew her hand. Her face almost immediately turned crimson with embarrassment. Stopping again, she covered her face with her hands.

I stopped walking too. I wasn't sure what to do. I could tell that with a few words, I had shattered any romantic delusions that she may have imagined. However, I still needed an ally in this world to assist me in accomplishing what I'd been drawn here for. Besides anything else, I still considered Mib to be my friend... *a true friend*. Reaching to her covered face, I drew one of her hands to mine again.

"My niece, Mib... and my friend," I added. "You are one of the few in this land who I know and trust. And you are the only best friend I've ever had. We still need to get your people to see what Gamious is doing to your society. If he is still in power as you have said, then the need to expose him for what he is has not changed in the past eight cycles. I need your help. We first of all have to rescue your father."

She looked at me for a long moment; eventually smiled the same girlish smile I remembered, and grabbed me in a bear hug before I realized what was happening! I was surprised, but it felt good to be hugged by Mib. It felt good to still have a friend.

Suddenly she broke off our embrace, rollicking in a fit of laughter. "I had a crush on my uncle!" she blurted out. "My uncle! Gross!" she said as she made a face like sour lemons. Gross was a word I had taught her during our former wanderings.

"Not necessarily gross," I countered as I struck a melodramatic pose. "I think you may have just been blinded by my stunning good looks!"

Her answer was a chorus of giggles. I feigned hurt feelings, and then enjoyed a long laugh with her.

"Well, Jeff," she continued as we tried to get our giggles under control, "I'm glad our friendship remains true." Then she smiled at me for a long moment before we ran to catch up with her brother and Ker-Lee.

Recognizing how beautiful Mib had become as a young woman, I regretted that we were related, and that I was now the younger one. Oh well, I thought, I'm glad I was at least nice to her when she was younger, especially now that our roles are reversed!

"Come on buddy!" she exclaimed, as she grabbed my hand to pull me along, "We have a journey to undertake, and a palace to conquer."

Mib's easy attitude and quick adaptability helped me to feel light-minded and happy. I momentarily forgot the pressures I had felt the past days as I had begun to accept my role as Deliverer; especially that of still not knowing what I was supposed to deliver these people from. Little did I know that each in our party were about to face the greatest challenges of our lives.

-CHAPTER SEVENTEEN-
Desolation of Innerland

A few hours later, as we approached West Reach, I began to understand what Mib meant when she said that there had been changes. Compared to my memories of the day before, the town was wasted! I suppose that the destruction might have come gradually, but my recollections from the day prior showed it to be quite different environmentally.

Stretching for kilometers, before and to the side of me, where lush old growth forests of pine had greeted me upon my first arrival, there now was only sparse vegetation. The sweet scent of the musk trees I had longed to breathe, after our hours of walking in the tunnels, was not to be had. Instead, a sour stink permeated the dank air. Rivers and canals continued to meander across the face of the land, however most had lost their crystalline hue, and now looked brackish and wasted. It even appeared that several of the sapphire lakes, which had dotted the landscape, were no longer even there.

The green glow of the walls was fainter than it should have been for the time of day that Mib said it was. It was as though the light itself was wearing out. Even when a light breeze kicked up, it did little but rearrange the smoke from an occasional noonses fire. I wished I could gain some reassurance by telling myself that it was merely a dream; yet this time I knew it was real. I felt a sudden anxiety to be Outside in the open air. What a contrast that lush land was to the desolation I now beheld. And finally, with that anxiety, came to me the reason that I was sent to deliver the people of Innerland. The contrast that I witnessed from one day to another (from my perspective) served more to reveal my purpose to me here than if I had remained and watched this gradual devastation of the environment occur over the last several cycles.

We meandered through the rubbish-strewn streets, eventually coming to the familiar looking three story home near the center of the town. Intricate woodworking on the posts surrounding the doorways that had once been covered with bright dyes and paints were now faded beyond the natural aging of eight cycles. The ivy that had once grown around the outside was withered and brown. The whole effect of the scene reminded me of an inner city slum.

Tabob could stand the contrast to the world he had just left no longer. With tears streaming down his contorted features, he turned to Mib. "What has happened to the home I knew, my sister?" he demanded, as he held her arms firmly. Though I didn't speak it, I wondered the same.

For long moments her only response was to echo Tabob's sorrow. The sadness in the air was tangible. Finally, Tabob pulled his sister to him, and we entered the home.

Though the outside had fallen to decay, the inside of the house was nearly as bright and welcoming as I'd last seen it. I was grateful to find something that seemed constant amidst the radical changes I was encountering since our return. The warm meal (though not as good as Miyab had cooked) was, nevertheless, satisfying after our jaunt from the Great Door. There were few meats or fruits. However, the dry supplies made a passing meal.

After our three guests were fed, Ker-Lee trussed them back up, and encouraged them to get some sleep as he locked them in a storage room.

The mood towards the unusually dark late afternoon turned uncomfortably sodden. The desolation we had seen on our journey in had dampened each of our spirits. Even gentle Mib, who I remembered being a lot more talkative, was silent. We lounged around in the sitting room feeling listless. I gradually grew tired, and fell asleep.

I didn't sleep soundly, or long, before I heard the cautiously muted voice of Mib. "Jeff? Come quietly." Mib and Tabob were already awake and alert. After waking me, Mib woke Ker-Lee. I could hear the voices of several men walking around outside. Pounce stirred from my lap, and I stroked his back to reassure him before placing him gently into the cowl of my jacket.

"Our prisoners?" I whispered as I stood.

"No," replied Tabob quietly. "Other guards. We were foolish to come back here, and then to stay for so long. But I have an idea. Follow me."

Obediently, we gathered our packs and stealthily followed Tabob's lead. We negotiated the passage below the eating room just as I heard the main door of the house forced open with a reverberating crunch. I lowered the trap door over the storage area, and then I turned in time to see Ker-Lee scrambling into the mouth of an opened barrel!

I looked questioningly at Tabob.

"No time to explain, Deliverer," he said, as he half pushed me into the mouth of the barrel after Ker-Lee.

How am I going to fit in this thing with him, I thought. *It's a big barrel, but he's a big man!*

But as I crawled, I didn't come to Ker-Lee, or the bottom of the barrel. Instead I emerged into a small room. Ker-Lee and Mib were there ahead of me. A dull thunk, then Tabob's head emerged from the barrel tunnel just behind me. He flashed a sly grin at me, which I returned as I patted him on the shoulder.

"You and Ker-Lee may have some surprises that can get us to my father, Deliverer, yet I've a few of my own too," declared Tabob as he led us into a small room. We were hidden behind a barrel in the food storage, beneath the eating chamber!

Tabob quietly pushed some sacks of grain back the way we had come, probably to fool any who might think to look in the barrel. Then he placed a false bottom across the entrance to the room we occupied. Tabob motioned for silence as we heard a distant clunk, signaling the descent of the guards into the storage chamber. It was as quiet and ominous as a tomb as we breathed shallowly, listening and hoping for our rue to work. We held our breath while the guards took an eternity to satisfy their searching. When it sounded as though they were about to move on to another part of the house, Pounce let out a low, moaning, whine! The game was up, and I knew we were caught.

The footsteps of one guard paused, as if he were listening. Though I knew our lives were in jeopardy, I couldn't harm Pounce in order to silence him. I knew he didn't understand the need for quiet, and the dark bothered him.

As we huddled in tense silence, the other guard laughed. "It's just a glib, or other some-such vermin. Since the trees have died out, many terrorize the storehouses of the citizens in the Reaches."

The first guard agreed with the second. "You're right. They must have cleared out already. Let's get out'a here; it's musty in this sub-room."

Slowly their laughter and footsteps receded up the stairs. At the final slamming of the cellar door we let out a collective sigh. We seemed to have passed one more trial unscathed. I hoped good fortune would continue with us.

When Tabob unsheathed a glow-bone, I realized that the room we were in was not just a single room, but also an entrance to what seemed to be an underground passageway system. As I looked questioningly at Tabob, he smiled, and said, "Not all slowlis are as big as the one who attacked you, you know!" As we walked, he explained that he and Vocata had found the tunnels when he was a young boy. "Vocata used them when he needed to contact another Ancient in secret, which happened more and more in the cycles since Gamious came to power. I also found them useful when I stayed out too long with my friends. It was as a way to get back into the house unnoticed." Mib just smiled at her big brother, and shook her head in mock disgust.

After walking a safe distance into the tunnels, when we were certain our voices didn't carry, we commenced to plan. Ker-Lee attested that my diagrams of the palace were still fairly accurate. It hadn't changed much in the nearly four hundred cycles since Dad had it constructed. However, he was able to clarify some minor changes: a new wall here, a door or window added there. Also, Ker-Lee's knowledge of the typical guard posting came in handy, after we had familiarized ourselves with the modified floor plan.

We decided on a route, and then surfaced amidst one of the few remaining clumps of greenery on the now barren landscape, amidst some small boulder outcroppings that were frequent in the area between West Reach and Highland. We stayed under cover until it was fully dark. We then continued carefully on our journey to Coreterior, intent on freeing Vocata.

The trip to the palace went without incident. We made good time too; it only took us about two and a half, maybe three hours. It wasn't nearly as fast as it had been my first trip, but certainly under much better circumstances. I was glad we made it when we did too, since my foot injury was becoming increasingly sore. Bad as it then seemed, I was grateful that Dad had the foresight to get me treatment while home. The artificial skin worked better than even Miyab's ointment, although the ointment (which I'd also included) came in handy to deaden the pain, and I applied some now.

"Let's look for the passage," I suggested after we had rested. While perusing the plans in my father's journal, we had identified a couple of escape passages that Ker-Lee said were not known to him. We had collectively decided on one that would lead us closest to where Mib said Vocata was being held, and we had about an hour before the guards were supposed to be changed.

The target area was an escape route that went under the palace foundations to a hall close by where Vocata was imprisoned. Our goal was to backtrack it, get Vocata, and get back out before he was missed. Once out, we would likely have a pretty good chance to escape into the wilderness area or hide out with one of the loyal Ancients.

Our proposed ingress lay near a rocky outcropping, above a steep ledge, overlooking a large subterranean lake south of the palace. The area, as we approached it, became dense with bushes and undergrowth, so we had to move quietly. Apparently the lands of Gamious had been spared the ravages that had been heaped upon Innerland in general.

I was in the lead, searching carefully in the near black of the night, when I heard a rustle several meters to the fore of our location. A guard, carrying a glow-bone, slowly rounded a corner of the palace. The exposed bone unleashed its blinding light on the black night. I had barely time to give silent warning for my companions to take cover before the beam of light from the skeletal remains of a cavern builder swept over our position. Fortunately, all of us had adequate time to crouch behind whatever natural cover that was available. The passing guard did not pause in his rounds, and was soon gone from sight. He hadn't seen us.

I moved from my hiding place slightly, in an attempt to communicate with the others. Placing my hand on some rubble, it unexpectedly gave way, and I leaned out into empty space momentarily, before plummeting after the rocks I had knocked loose. I had just time to think I had accidentally gone the wrong way and fallen off of the ledge which overlooked the lake, when I hit the ground with a thud. As I regained my breath, I realized that my first conclusion was wrong, and that I had somehow stumbled into a hole or a cavern. *A cavern?*

I quickly crawled back up to the opening. "Psst."

"Jeff?" called Mib tentatively.

"Get the others. I found the escape tunnel."

We were all soon safely inside the shaft. A relatively short hike later, and we were inside of an apparently little used storage room near the bottom of the palace. Mib led the way, and we encountered no more guards on our way to her father's quarters.

Before I knew it, we were in the room where Vocata was being held. I could barely believe our luck; we had encountered no resistance and very little in the way of close calls. I believed that good fortune was with us, but so far it had been almost too easy for a fortress that was supposed to be impregnable.

Tabob uncovered the glow-bone he always carried, and made a sweep of the room. No one besides us was currently there. Next we uncovered the wall sconces that held glow-bones. Still nothing. I was beginning to get nervous, and a little frustrated.

"I thought you said you visited your father just two days ago," I stated, trying to hide my growing frustration.

"Yes," Mib replied simply.

"Then where is he, Sister?" Tabob queried, failing to hide his growing stress at the situation just as much as I had.

"I don't understand!" exclaimed an exasperated Mib. "This was his room. He must be here!"

"Sorry to disappoint you, Missy," came an unknown voice from behind. Whirling around, we found ourselves facing five well-armed guards, three with crossbows leveled at us—I didn't think ducking would save me this time! The leader of the group wore the black leather arm protection of a head-guard. Additionally, his chest bore the same type of shimmering oval orb that had once nearly cost me my life. When I looked into the one worn by Corun I was hypnotized. This time I steeled my glare on the guard's eyes, rather than his breastplate.

"Don't try to fight them," warned Ker-Lee before any of us could act. "These are better trained soldiers than the guards we tackled at the cave. These are the Center Judge's elite."

"You'd best listen to the turncoat, children. Though his loyalties are inaccurate, his appraisal of the situation is not. Besides, as you can see," the spokesman said as he waved his arm with a flourish towards the three armed with crossbows, "If you try to fight, at least some will die, as these men have excellent aim. At this range, it would be no contest even if these soldiers were not well trained.

Now turn around!" he bellowed. "Gamious seeks audience with you, as he expected you to try something this foolish."

No wonder getting in here was such a cinch, I thought, regretting not having suspected a trap before now. The four of us, seeing no recourse at present, turned around as instructed. Our plan had been so good too, and had gone along nearly perfectly! As I felt the pointed tip of the crossbow bolt wedged uncomfortably into the small of my back, and was forced to march with the others, all I could think was, *This isn't how it happens in the comics!*

-CHAPTER EIGHTEEN-
A Costly Escape

Caught! Gamious had second-guessed us, and had somehow known that we would try to spirit Vocata out from under his nose. Yet, we hadn't even seen Vocata yet! If what the guard had said was true (about the Judge knowing our intentions) then Vocata had likely been moved long before we even arrived. The four of us were escorted towards the door of the room, to exit into a hallway where more guards probably awaited. I desperately wanted to try something, anything, to get away. Once we were in the hallway there would be even less of a chance of escape. Curly had warned us that our captors were better trained than the fellows we had bested at the Inner Door. Besides, even if these soldiers weren't very good shots, how good of an aim do you have to be to hit a target at point blank range? Then, quite abruptly, as my mind was racing to come up with a plan of escape, our captors stopped walking.

"What are you doing?" I demanded, as I felt the tip of the bolt slowly backed away from my skin. "Well?" I persisted.

My only answer was the sound of several simultaneous thuds, as many large objects hit the floor behind us. I whirled around to see Vocata standing there, flanked by two other elderly gentlemen. Each held a glowing staff pointed in our direction; the same as Vocata had used against Corun when he attacked me in the alley ages ago. The guards, who had moments before held us captive, lay prone on the floor, stiff, and unconscious.

Vocata smiled in greeting as he held his arms wide in a half circle. "Jeff. My children. It is good to see you all again"

"But how did you...?" My question trailed off amidst my fascination before it could be asked.

Sensing what I was about to inquire, Vocata continued to smile, and said, "Gamious may have taken the political power of title from the Ancients, but our true mastery remains intact." He held up his glowing staff for emphasis.

His two companions smiled wryly at him, and then stepped respectfully to the side as Tabob, Mib, and myself rushed forward and embraced Vocata. Ever the warrior, Ker-Lee first removed the weapons of our five disabled opponents, and then secured their hands behind their backs. Tabob and I pulled away from embracing his father in time to help Ker-Lee gag the still unconscious guards. Securing the door, we talked briefly.

"It was good fortune indeed that brought you children here to rescue me. And at the same time my fellow Ancients, Junada and Sefas, were attempting a similar plan," kidded Vocata as he pointed to his smiling friends. "Jeff, I am glad to see you have returned. As well as you, Son," he added, as he nodded towards Tabob. Then he continued, "Since you have returned to us from Otherworld, I suppose you talked with your father?" he queried of me.

"Our father, you mean," I corrected him with a slight smile. "But I still find it difficult to accept that my kid brother is an old man named Vocata," I joked.

"As it is for me to believe that my older brother, a man possessing wisdom beyond his cycles, is still trapped in the body of a boy," he countered. Then he abruptly asked, "The Stone?"

Pulling it out from under my shirt, I dangled the velvety, black talisman before his eyes.

"I cannot see far into the future," Vocata continued, "But I think we will succeed now that you, Jeff, and the Stone of Recognition, have both been returned to us." Vocata's two ancient looking companions nodded in agreement, unaccustomed smiles decorating their wizened features.

"Where is Mother?" questioned Mib suddenly.

"Don't worry, little one," assured Vocata as he gently placed his hand on her shoulder. "Miyab left yesterday. As you know, she stayed here of her own choice, to be near me. I was the only one compelled to remain here. She now waits for us in safety"

"We need to go quickly," urged Junada, the shorter of his two companions.

"Quite so," agreed Vocata. "This guard is a friend, Jeff?" he asked me, gesturing towards Ker-Lee.

"Yes," I assured him, "Ker-Lee is a loyal friend. He helped us find our way here."

"You probably know your way around the palace pretty well then, Ker-Lee?"

"Yes, sir," he responded in curt, military fashion.

"Since you also wear the garb of a guard, you would probably be the best one to go ahead of the party, in case we meet any unexpected guests. Would you agree, Jeff?" asked Vocata. I knew his way was the best plan, yet he still deferred to me. Perhaps so that others would know that Vocata looked to me as the Deliverer also. I appreciated that. It would probably come in handy to have the loyal support of my brother later, when we met with all of the Ancients.

"Yes," I agreed hastily. "We need to stop delaying and get out before we're discovered." My brother's deference was appreciated, but I didn't feel we had time to waste.

Following Ker-Lee, we kept to the shadows of the lower level and headed for the escape tunnel we had entered in through. Gamious' plan to have the halls pretty much deserted in order to lure us here also proved his undoing: there was really no one to stop us from leaving either, once the guards in the room had been taken care of. We made good time and all was going along well until we were just a couple of halls away from the storage closet that hid our escape route.

We heard the footfalls of several men approaching. They walked at a normal pace, so we had time for all of our party to become secreted in an unused room prior to their arrival. All, that is, except for Ker-Lee. The remainder of our small party pressed against the inside of the tiny room we were hiding in. I listened in on the conversation in the hallway, and secretly hoped that Ker-Lee was as good an actor as he was a soldier.

"What are you doing here?" came the voice of the new arrival. "I don't recognize you, Guard, and I've been assigned to the palace as Third Head Counselor for five cycles. Besides, Judge Gamious has ordered these hallways clear tonight, he-"

"Sir! Begging your pardon," Ker-Lee cut in, "The friends of Vocata, the ones Gamious planned the trap for, they are here!"

Had my trust been unfounded? Had Ker-Lee betrayed us?

"What?" exclaimed the Third Head Counselor.

"I was part of the five man team sent to trap the intruders. But they are more numerous than we thought: We are outnumbered five to one! Quick, bring all of your men before they escape. No time to talk, we need reinforcements!"

Ker-Lee sounded very convincing. A few seconds later, and the footfalls of the host of guards receded into the distance. As we were coming out to continue towards the escape passage, Ker-Lee came slyly around the corner.

"It's OK" he assured us, "They outran me on the way to fight the twenty-five of you," he laughed. Then added, "I shouldn't be missed for a few moments yet."

We didn't stop to enjoy the joke right then. Rather, we ran to the escape passageway, and made double time to the outside ledge we had come in through. We hadn't been among the thick bushes at the south portion of the palace long, when there suddenly came a cry from the watchtower, "Assemble the troops! The intruders have escaped!"

"What now, little brother?" I whispered to Vocata, as I caught his arm.

"Now our part of the escape plan comes into play, Deliverer," replied Sefas, the taller of Vocata's companions, before my brother had a chance to consider a response. He made the chattering cry of a glib, authentic sounding enough that even Pounce sat up and took notice. We immediately saw several figures stand up in the distance, by the cliff ledge that overlooked the Great Lake. "Come," encouraged Sefas simply.

Vocata's lanky friend led us to the very edge of the cliff, among six or seven other men. I couldn't see them well, but they seemed to be younger. Their escape plan soon became evident. Moored below us, on the surface of the immense lake, was a small armada of boats. The young men standing by the edge let drop several knotted rope ladders, which we in turn mounted and began descending. Junada and Sefas, the two ancients who had also attempted to rescue Vocata, were lowered in baskets to their awaiting boats. Yet Vocata, who was clearly older than the other two Ancients, shinnied down the rope ladder the same as the rest of us. Iamb was right: even at his great age, Vocata was a spry man.

We were away a few moments before the guards appeared over the top of the bluff. Then I noticed that the rope ladders were still dangling off of the precipice! Hadn't they noticed? The pursuing soldiers could climb down as easily as we just had.

In sudden panic, I turned to the young man rowing next to me. "What about the ladders?" I asked, "The guards will be coming down any second!"

He paused in his rowing for just a moment, and pointed to the base of the cliff we had just left. "They will be down soon, you are right. But they cannot swim as fast as we can row!" he laughed as he began to row again. In the dim early first light of morning, I saw the flotsam and jetsam of what had probably been ten times the number of boats we now occupied, floating uselessly near the shoreline. The Ancients had sunken the fleet of Gamious! It was plain the soldiers would not be following us the same way we had left.

    I settled down to enjoy the ride. We were all arranged in the various boats (I counted seven) and had pushed off towards the other side of the lake. As the pursuing soldiers reached the cliff edge, the first line dropped and let loose a volley of arrows. I thought we might be far enough away to be safe. A pair of screams sounded from a nearby boat as two arrows found their marks. Next, a groan came from behind me.

    I pushed my way into the fallen row-man's seat to lend my muscle, and hopefully put a greater distance between our little group and the range of that flying death. The Archers let their arrows loose again. Several more screams. Our small group was being cut to ribbons on the open water. The walls, several kilometers in the distance and on all sides, began to glow brighter now, signaling dawn in Innerland. I pulled harder on my oar. A scream from another boat as another arrow found its mark. I pulled back hard again on the oar I manned.

    Mib screamed my name from the boat nearest me. "Jeff!"

    I turned and directed my gaze, not towards her, but back in the way of the archers who still fired on us. A high-pitched whistling sound, a single shaft headed towards my upturned face...

    Then, the shaft abruptly stopped. The arrow did not glide off path; it just stopped in mid-air, mere centimeters from my nose! It hung there motionless for an entire moment, and then fell vertically, to land harmlessly on the floor of the boat. The Stone of Recognition was glowing beneath my shirt. Another volley of arrows, then a groan from the boat nearest me as Mib pitched forward, an arrow protruding from her inert form.

    What happened next, could only have been caused by instinct. I say this because I didn't really think about what I did. The thought came, and with the thought came instantaneous action. In one fluid movement, as the boat bobbed unsteadily beneath me, I lurched to my feet, pulled the amulet from beneath my shirt, held it upright, and screamed a single word. "STOP!" My solitary word echoed, and then all fell momentarily silent.

The Stone glowed with a light that shone through my hand. A bolt of physical warmth and heat shot from my extended fist towards the assembling army on the bluff. It connected with them with a resounding boom that knocked me to my seat, and caused all of the boats to rock unsteadily upon the sudden waves. The cliff face was obliterated. Gone. Dust clouds hung tenaciously on as rocks fell regularly into the dirge. The remaining army could be seen retreating up the farther slopes, back towards the palace.

I stood, transfixed as I thought about what I had just caused to happen. That is, what the Stone had just allowed me to do… then, noticing the open-mouthed gapes and stares of my companions, instinct took over for me again. I stepped across the space between my boat and the one Mib was riding in. She was unconscious, yet still breathed. I held her hand as Junada applied a poultice and attempted to dislodge the arrow. "Come," I spoke above the overwhelming silence, "Tend to our wounded, and let's continue on our planned journey."

Obediently, the masters of the boats directed their rowers to continue on. I sat down, still deep in contemplation of the miracle I had just witnessed, a miracle that had happened through me. We were nearly overcome, and then...

How had I known to do what I just did? Had I read something in my father's journal that had prompted the action? And then, in my contemplations, I realized that some greater good was working its purposes through me to help lead this people away from the dregs which Gamious and his followers had rewarded them.

We would gather: the ancients with their loyal followers, my newfound family, and me. Then I would propose the plan of deliverance that had been forming in my mind since first witnessing the desolation of this once beautiful land yesterday morning. I thought upon how I might present my ideas to Vocata's people, as I continued to hold Mib's hand and listen to her irregular breathing.

-CHAPTER NINETEEN-
Gathering of Ancients

We were safely secreted for the moment in Central Reach; a mid-sized city located between Coreterior and Highland. Our little party had successfully spirited Vocata away from the palace of the Great Center Judge Gamious, where he had been interred for the last eight cycles. We were able to elude the guard patrols by following several small tributaries, finally landing, and disguising ourselves as part of a merchant caravan.

Towards the end of the first day we made it to the rendezvous that the Ancients had selected with Vocata. Our passage, however, was not without losses: three young men had died from wounds sustained during our escape. Several more were wounded, including Mib, who had not yet regained consciousness. The Ancients, who I was informed were the best healers in Innerland, continued to work with her, as they did with the other wounded. We found Miyab there; she helped attend her wounded daughter. Even knowing that Mib was in capable hands, my concern for her was nearly overwhelming.

All of us were currently housed in the great hall of Junada (the short, tense Ancient that had been in on the rescue of Vocata last night) along with various others who had assembled for the upcoming meeting. Vocata had spread the word that a Deliverer had come among the people. Stories of the power I had shown at the palace, using the Stone of Recognition, had already been circulated and elaborated on. The Council of the Ancients was to be held shortly, and I was to address them. Vocata and I visited briefly before the meeting began.

"How fares Mib?" he asked me, though I knew he was as aware of her condition as I was. I'm certain he could also sense my concern, so he gave me an opportunity to talk about her.

"Her condition has improved little. The arrow has been removed though, and it was not poisoned. Your wife is still with her," I replied, almost mechanically. I wanted to do something for Mib, but I didn't understand what that could be.

"What is your plan, Deliverer," asked Vocata. "I ask so that I will know how I can best support you when your ideas are presented."

"You will support me, without even knowing what my plan is?" I asked my newfound brother in surprise.

"Jeff, when we talked briefly yesterday, I teased that my brother was a wise man trapped inside the body of a boy. However, I really meant it. I have often thought it strange, how the times between our worlds do not match. Jeff, even though when we have finally met I appear to you to be an old man, you are still my older brother."

"When our father returned to Innerland and talked with me as a boy, two cycles after our mother had passed away, he told me of an older brother named Jeffrey. I idolized you, Jeff. I imagined what you would be like, and hoped that your coming in the role of Deliverer would happen during my lifetime so that I might meet the big brother I revered while growing up. When Father returned, each time after an eight year cycle had passed, I realized that I would likely grow old, live my life, and be gone before you were called into our world. I wanted so for it to be otherwise. I was thrilled that day, cycles ago, when you turned up on my doorstep with Tabob. I didn't know the reason you had come then. Now, I do know the reason. I believe your plan probably has something to do with ridding the land of the evil of Gamious. Whatever your plan is, I will follow it, for I have seen the evil he has heaped on our once great land. I have waited long to meet you, Jeff, and to follow you. I now anxiously await your word. I promise to follow what you propose. I defer to your greater wisdom. Be aware that some of the other Ancients will likely express pessimism because of your age. Many others will follow you, even though a youth, when they see me following you."

I was touched by the sincerity and loyalty of the brother I had never known until now, the brother that claimed to have idolized me for a lifetime. I outlined for Vocata the specifics of the plan I was still forming in my mind. As I shared my ideas, his eyes burned bright with anticipation. From the excitement that rode his features, I knew I would have his support; not just out of loyalty, but from a sense of adventure that burned within him as it likewise did in me. My parents had spawned a pair of dreamers. As we discussed details of my plan, I began to believe that it was a dream that could be turned into reality.

The time for the great meeting of the Ancients arrived. Vocata led me into a large room, located a level below the structure of the main house. Seated around an immense, odd shaped table, was an equally large and curious assortment of old men, and women. I don't mean to be chauvinistic, but I hadn't realized until then that Ancients were women too. All I had seen previously of the Ancients were Vocata, and the other old guys he hung around with. Yet, about a third of those assembled were female Ancients.

Vocata had barely introduced me as the Deliverer when a challenge rang out.

"If this boy is really the Deliverer, let's see the Stone!"

Cries of "The Stone! The Stone!" suddenly rang out from all corners of the room.

Vocata nodded to me. Pulling it from under the covering of my shirt, I dangled the black talisman before the startled eyes of those assembled. Sudden and complete silence filled the chamber.

"Now," continued a disgusted Vocata, "I hope we will each behave more as Ancients, and less like unruly school children." No arguments from the silent assemblage. "Even though Gamious has removed our political titles, we still retain our true power. Let us in dignity act the part of-"

The same fellow who had previously started the chanting (a skinny old guy with long, oily hair, and an unusually pointed nose) rudely interrupted Vocata. The guy's hair looked as though he had painted it black in places. Even so, the dingy grey showed through. When he spoke, it was as if he were whining. "That's what it's about, isn't it? Gamious. Is this a plot to kill him? Because if it is, I fail to see how we will be any better off with the Center Judge dead than we are now. Gamious' death will not bring the trees back."

The guy immediately grated on my nerves. I didn't like how he was trying to turn the group against our plan before they had even heard it. Using a boldness I didn't know I had, I addressed him. "No one is talking about killing Gamious. If we were to do that, we could consider ourselves no better than him and his henchmen."

"Then restore the environment for us," demanded a dignified elderly woman. She reminded me of the Queen of England.

"I don't believe that is what I have been sent to do at this time, ma'am," I respectfully countered. "The environment can't continue to support the demands that you have become accustomed to taking from it. It needs a rest, or it will completely die away."

"Then how can you deliver us, boy?" Greasy-Head again.

"By leaving Gamious and his scum to rot in the rubbish trap they've created. And taking the rest that will follow to a fresh land," I replied.

"There is nowhere else!" This objection came from the Queen of England look-a-like. "Even the unexplored lands are not thought big enough to feed all of Innerland. This is ridiculous, and a waste of time. I'm leaving!" As the elderly woman who objected (and several others) got up to leave, the Stone began to glow on its own, until it shone brightly, even from under my shirt. As various people noticed, the chattering quieted, until the room was again silent. Those who had stood remained still, and stared curiously at the Stone.

Having everyone's attention, I felt impressed that it was time to present my plan. "A wise teacher once told me that in order to solve problems, you need to 'see what no one else has ever seen, and try what no one else has ever tried.' " Mr. Measer, my math teacher, would be honored, hearing me quote him like this! "You people have become lazy! You have lived your lives within Innerland, eaten the fruit of its land, and thought that it would always be able to support you, without much thought of what you might give it in return. Well now, thanks to the despot Gamious and his mining operations, the time of your decision has been hurried a bit."

"Because you have allowed your forests to be destroyed, in order to fuel the Judge's insatiable hunger for precious metals, your world is nearly used up. The days are not as bright as you once remembered. The air is not as sweet. The gurgling, rushing streams have turned into stagnant ditchwater. Your children do not have the promise of a sweet and carefree life like you and your parents enjoyed. Gamious, and each of you by your permissiveness, have taken that from them. No matter what Gamious tells you, it will not get better by itself. It cannot at this point in time." I paused for a moment, hoping to give time for my words to sink in. Then I continued, "But I offer you another chance. Not an easy out, but a chance to live elsewhere, while Innerland repairs itself... A time to learn to care for your world; time that you have no more of in Innerland."

"But there is nowhere else." The same objection again.

"Nowhere else you say? That is the comment of one who has not thought a new thought in many cycles, who is afraid to try what has not been tried." I countered.

"Then where do you propose we go to? It is known that Inlanders cannot live long in Otherworld. The last Deliverer showed us that when his bride had to return after living for a time in your world."

I thought then upon my mother. I thought upon the ample space in the land from which her people had originally come. The land I had seen. Then, I trusted my feelings, as she had told me to do. "I offer each Inlander that which they may have thought existed only in legend. I offer... each of you... the bounty of Outside."

In the short time-span after my mention of the word Outside, I received a myriad of reactions. They ran the gambit from shock and surprise, to hope and vision, to laughter and derision. It does not take much guessing to determine whom the latter response came from: Greasy Head himself.

The objector approached me now in front of the entire assembly, paused momentarily, and then screamed, "You offer us bedtime tales, boy!" He stood as erect as he could manage, staring down his extended nose at me.

"I offer you deliverance from the squalor you have allowed to come upon your people, Sir," I countered, meeting his gaze squarely.

Vocata stepped between us. "I motion that a vote be taken. We should each take the proposition of the Deliverer to our various delegations, discuss its merits with our people, and return for a final decision in two day's time. Those favoring?"

About two-thirds of the hands were raised, some reluctantly.

"Those not favoring?"

The remainder held their hands vertically. We had won a respite, but it was not yet conclusive that the Inlanders would follow my idea. Well, I had presented my plan. However, with Mr. Grease trying to discredit my ideas before the Council of Ancients, I began to wonder if my plan would be accepted. I wished he would listen. I wished they all would listen. I now understood that the reason I was sent to Innerland was to lead these people to Outside.

Iamb, I thought, as those assembled rose to begin their departures, *I need you to help these people see that I tell the truth about Outside.* I wished the slowlis had told me how I might contact him in case of need. It occurred to me that the elderly leaders might place more faith in the words of a legendary monster than ideas coming from a teen-aged boy.

When Vocata and I were the only ones left in the room, he put his hand gently on my shoulder, and said, "That didn't go too badly."

"Compared to what?" I asked in disbelief.

"Compared to your escape attempt last night," he joked. I smiled, and then we both laughed loud and long. Our laughter was as much an attempt to alleviate the tension we both shared, as it was a response to anything funny that had been said. After all, my brother's joke hadn't been that funny.

"Let's go check on my daughter," Vocata suggested, as he put his arm around my shoulders and led me from the darkening room.

We passed Greasy-Head on our way out. The hall was bustling with preparations for the quick journey to the homelands of the Ancients.

"We will see you in two days, Jori," remarked Vocata to Greasy on our way by.

"Two days will not make any difference, Vocata," he replied in his whiny tone. My brother didn't notice the look of contempt that Jori (Mr. Grease) shot our way as we meandered by him on our way to Mib's room.

* * *

Two of our party, who had sustained wounds similar to Mib's, were both now conscious and eating. However, one of the other fellows had died while we were in the big meeting. There was, as yet, no improvement in Mib's condition. She was still unconscious, and had now come down with a fever. Everything that had seemed so clear and positive just the day before now seemed dark and muddled. I began to wrestle with a new foe as I got ready for bed that evening: fear.

Junada (who had, by the way, supported me with his vote) had been gracious enough to allow us to remain at his home that evening. He had also allowed several of the Ancients to rest there before beginning their various journeys in the morning. My bed wasn't as nice as the one I had slept in at Vocata's; it was just a cot. But I didn't complain; it was a place to sleep, and I felt fairly secure staying there. Vocata, Tabob, Ker-Lee and I bunked in the same room. Miyab and Mib were in the room adjacent. Pounce remained with Mib, as he had since she had been wounded the day before.

I heard some movement from Mib's room and some chattering from Pounce as I hovered between sleep and wakefulness. I stirred. Miyab must be up and about. Surely she would inform us as to any change in Mib's condition. After a few moments of hearing no more movement, and realizing that Pounce had quieted down, I drifted off to sleep.

My rest was not long enjoyed, however. I was awakened by muffled sounds coming from the direction of Vocata's and Tabob's cots. I sat up quickly, pushing my coverings to the floor.

"Vocata? Uunnngh-" I had started to speak to check on my friends. That action was interrupted by someone slugging me in the stomach with such force that it knocked the wind out of me. I listened to furtive whispers as my stomach reeled and a bag was forced over my head. A rope secured my arms before I even had a chance to catch my breath. I had difficulty breathing, and I began to kick at my captors as I felt a sudden panic that I would suffocate. My struggles were useless. I briefly felt a wet sensation in my mouth, as a rag soaked in a sickly sweet liquid was pressed to my face. As my muscles involuntarily relaxed, and I began to lose consciousness, I thought it peculiar that someone had taken such unusual exception to the speech I had given earlier. Strange and disquieting dreams soon joined me amidst my unnatural slumber.

-CHAPTER TWENTY-
Absurdity of Gamious

As the bag was removed from my head, and I became a little more coherent, I found myself in a familiar looking room. I looked over and saw Vocata, and realized that we were in a room at the palace! Tabob, Miyab, and Ker-lee had also been invited along. Mib was there too, still unconscious. Her mother had already moved over to her side. My bonds were cut, and I was allowed to stand along with the others. Massaging the feeling back into my limbs, I noticed that our gear was also here with us.

Gamious strolled over to me. "You age well boy," he mocked. Circling me, he continued, "You don't look a day older than when I last saw you, the day you were sentenced to die! You've probably not grown up much since then either. Still throwing rocks at carriages, or has your bag of tricks increased any beyond that?"

I didn't respond to his rambling. Instead, I wandered over to my pack and sat down by it. As Gamious continued his mocking tirade, I inconspicuously reached inside of my pack and pressed a familiar red button. However, Corun saw my hand as I quickly pulled it back.

"What are you doing?" he demanded, as he walked my direction.

"Nothing," I replied innocently, as I put my hands on my lap.

"Move back with the others." He waved with his spear. I complied. Corun then picked up my pack, moved over by the chair on which Gamious had sat down, and plopped my bag by the side of the Judge. Gamious sat on a dais, so that everyone in the room had to look up at him.

"The Inlanders are worried about the forests, aren't they boy?" Gamious questioned me.

I continued to ignore him. Atten, his chief guard, reached over and hefted me to my feet, wrenching my arm painfully as he did so.

"Answer the Judge, Boy!" his henchman spat at me. His breath was rivaled only by Iamb's.

Another twist of my arm by Atten, and I reluctantly answered Gamious. "Yes, they are concerned. With good reason," I added, "Your mining has- Unghnn-" I broke off mid sentence as Atten levered my arm vertically.

"Trees. Ah yes, they have a certain quaint beauty, Boy. I'll admit that. But have you ever looked upon gold? Now there's beauty!" At the mention of gold, he withdrew into himself for a few moments, stood up and began pacing the dais like a caged animal. Coming out of his reverie, he looked around at us, almost surprised that we were still there. Then he shook his head and continued. "A few cycles before you came to Innerland, before my power was as great as it is now," he paused to smirk at me, "I came upon a secret room while wandering the halls of the palace, late one evening. My insomnia that night led me to the greatest discovery of my lifetime. Behind a wall hanging, one that I had passed countless times, I noticed a detail I had never before seen. The stones in one spot were not joined as tightly together as the others in the wall. Upon examination, I discovered a secret door. After opening the door, I found the secret study of Toam-Azz, the one responsible for building the palace hundreds of cycles before. Imagine that: it had been there for so many cycles, yet I had never noticed it. Judging by the dust, no one else had either, at least not since the builder last shut the room.

"I found books, many books. I returned often and read them during the course of the next several nights. Most of the writings were superstitious drivel about the history of Deliverers. But in one volume, Toam-Azz referred to the metal gold. His description of the metal fascinated me! I had never seen or heard of gold before that. He wrote that during the quarrying of the stone for this fortress, in a certain site, he had come across a vein of the precious metal. None of the other workers had noticed, so he covered it up after taking a small sample. Upon testing that sample, he found that it was, indeed, the gold metal of which he spoke. I found his sample in a little vial on the shelf where he had placed it himself, undisturbed for all of those cycles. He and his wife, a foolish Inlander, decided that it would be best if the people never knew about the metal, so the palace stones were quarried at various other places throughout Innerland. However, I had found his record, and by his descriptions, easily found the abandoned quarry he had referred to. It was then a simple matter to deploy servants to search for the metal. Though it took several cycles, we eventually found it."

I looked around at his head guard's garb, and the accessories he wore. I understood now where the gold talismans had come from, as well as the other gaudy decorations of his elite troops.

Gamious' voice rose as he continued, uninterrupted, on his tirade. He got more excited with each uttered syllable. "Workers under my command eventually came up with sophisticated machines that could get the gold for me more quickly. The cost of a few workers' lives and the exhausting of the musk trees as a source of fuel, were both unfortunate consequences. But… I got more gold. More gold! The amount that lay hidden beneath the surface of Innerland was more vast than even the foolish Toam-Azz could have guessed!"

Whirling around the room now, Gamious pulled down wall hanging after wall hanging, exposing intricately detailed rectangular pictures, each depicting scenes from Innerland, which had been fashioned from the gold he had unearthed. Last of all he paused, and with great reverence pulled the last hanging from behind the chair he had sat upon, revealing the largest gold-wrought picture of all. The light from the accumulated reflection was so bright I had to shield my eyes. From the newly uncovered picture, larger than life, leered the visage of Gamious. I gazed in amazement at the portrait. It looked more handsome than he now was. More like when I had first seen him, cycles ago. The comparison of the two showed that the passing of time had warped the man before me, into something much less now than he once was.

"Jef-Re, Vocata, and other guests," he continued, "Don't you see? Long after Innerland has heaved its last death throe, even an eternity from now, I will still live, because of gold! Gold! GOLD!" he laughed as he twirled around, the reflected light dancing off of his maddened features.

"You're mad," was all I could muster.

"Perhaps," he smiled, as he stopped his eccentric dance to look at me. And then, in a singsong voice, he added, "But I'll still be a-live to-mor-row…"

"Why have you brought our gear?" asked Tabob.

"You always were a bit dull witted compared to your older brother Corun," responded Gamious with a condescending chuckle. "But since you will all soon pass into history, I will share my plan with you. You all left the council last night. Yes, that's it. The other Ancients will realize that you all went on your supercilious quest without them. Your bodies, or what remains of them, will be found in a week or so. Killed, oh yes, by a slowlis. It was your destiny Jef-Re," he said as he looked down his nose and sneered at me. "Did you really think you'd get away? I don't think so." Then he walked over to Mib and stood over her prone figure. Miyab, who still held her daughter, looked in grief at the face of the monster Gamious who continued his charade as a man.

"Since she is nearly dead already, she will be the first to die by the hands of the slowlis." Gamious quickly pulled out his gold-coated sheath-knife, and before we could make any move to intercept him, had sunk it deep into the breast of the now inert form of Mib.

This could not be happening: Gamious had just killed my best friend! In shock, I did nothing but gaze in utter disbelief upon the scene that unfolded before my eyes. It was like the dreams I had after being drugged and kidnapped to this place.

Miyab's aged body was racked with sobs as she pulled her daughter's lifeless body close to her bosom.

Gamious laughed insanely.

Vocata ran for Gamious, who continued giving vent to the evil laugh I had first heard when he passed a death sentence on me at the palace. Before Vocata could get to him, he was knocked to the floor by Atten, and ceased moving.

Gamious continued to laugh insanely, and was joined in turn by his chief guard.

Tabob screamed his battle cry, "West Reach!" and lunged weaponless at his brother Corun. Corun in turn smiled silently, unsheathed his sword, and cut his younger brother down to the ground. Tabob shuddered, and joined his sister in everlasting stillness.

Our three captors continued to laugh insanely as Gamious grabbed a screaming Pounce from Mib's lifeless form, and hurtled our pet, still screeching, into one of the panels of gold that adorned the walls. The sickening impact stilled my little friend.

The Stone of Recognition hummed to me from beneath my shirt. I could feel its soft warmth, comforting even in these circumstances. Instinct took over for me again. But what I did was not very heroic. For some reason, I clutched the Stone of Recognition. But instead of a violent backlash, as at the cliff a morning ago, I fell to my knees, surveyed the scene around me, and uttered in despair a few simple words. "No... It's not supposed to happen this way." Then I fell forward into a heap, and sobbed uncontrollably.

* * *

[Deliverer.]

I lifted my head and stared into the tear-strewn face of Iamb. Nothing else was around us. Nothing. Just the gentle feel of Iamb's rumbly voice in my mind, and his mournful countenance.

[Gaze upon the terror that waits for all of Innerland, Deliverer. With your looking, get wisdom. Change the inheritance that Gamious would bequeath for all Inlanders.]

And then, he too, was gone.

* * *

"...all left the council. Yes, that's it. They will realize that you went on your supercilious quest without them. What are you bawling for boy?" asked Gamious.

I looked up at him, and then around the room. Tears were still streaming down my face. Tabob and Vocata were standing across from me as they had been a few moments ago... I quickly looked over at Mib. Miyab still held her daughter leaning on her lap. Mib was unconscious, but she was breathing! The Stone had shifted time in reverse for a few moments. I hoped, beyond hope, that a few moments would be all I would need.

"Crying will not change the inevitable, Boy," scolded Gamious.

It will, if I can help it, I thought at him in defiance.

Ignoring me, Gamious spoke again. "Your bodies, or what remains of them, will be found in a week or so. Killed, oh yes, by a slowlis. It was your destiny, Jef-Re," he said as he looked down his nose at me. "Did you really think you'd get away? I don't think so." Then he walked over to Mib and stood over her prone figure.

I knew I needed to act, but the time was still not yet. I felt I would burst, but the Stone held me frozen. I couldn't witness this scene again!

"Since she is nearly dead already, she will be the first to die-"

Then, I knew what to do, and acted in the same instant that I understood.

"Gamious," I stated, my voice slowly rising, as he unsheathed his knife and drew it down upon the defenseless form of Mib, "You and yours will trouble Innerland no more!" Deliberately holding aloft the

Stone of Recognition, several slender beams of warm, blinding white light struck out, one each at Gamious, Atten, Corun, and each of the other guards assembled. The streams of light from the Stone blazed at each of our foes for a moment, then stopped with a slight electronic sizzle as abruptly as they had commenced. Gamious and his henchmen each fell in turn to the floor. They were alive, but far from conscious.

* * *

At Vocata's urging, we snuck into the Chamber of the Ancients before the predetermined time for the meeting. "There is a traitor among the Ancients, and we must detect him before our exodus from Innerland," Vocata had warned. His plan seemed wise, so we secreted ourselves and waited for the Ancients to gather. When they were finally all seated a few hours later, the still greasy haired Jori, presumed it upon himself to conduct the meeting.

"I regret to inform you that Vocata, and his pretended Deliverer, as well as his family and friends, have deserted us. Presumably because they thought they could not rally support for their fantasy trip to a mythical Outside." Some laughter from those assembled. "They only sought to deceive us, and discredit Gamious, who has done so much good for our world."

It looked as though we had our traitor. I supposed this was my cue. Vocata must have had the same idea, because we simultaneously stepped from behind the curtains on opposite sides of the room. Jori's mouth fell open, and all color drained from his face, as his, and the eyes of all assembled looked at Vocata and me.

I held up the tape recorder. "The words of your crazed master, Jori," I said as I pressed play on the little machine Dad had insisted I bring along. I played the tape in its entirety, to the amazement of all assembled. <...long after Innerland has heaved its last death throe, even an eternity from now, I will still live, because of gold! Gold! GOLD...>

As the tape finished, Jori attempted to mumble an excuse. Tabob and a grinning Ker-Lee then ushered in Gamious, Atten, and Corun, hands bound. Vocata's words cut off any further apologies by Jori.

"Who now will follow the Deliverer to the clean lands of Outside?" The vote was unanimously in favor of my plan. Even Jori voted in favor of it, though I'm not sure whether his vote counted or not.

"Then this has now turned into a court of the Ancients," continued Vocata. "We, as the true government of Innerland, in the presence of our Deliverer, must decide as to a sentence to be passed on these four individuals who have not only poisoned our land, but the spirits and minds of all Inlanders as well."

The trial did not last long. The Ancients were far more generous with Gamious and company than he would have been with any of them. It goes to prove that the Ancients were, ultimately, a better breed of people than Gamious was, and more suitable to lead the people. Gamious and his three buddies, including Vocata's eldest son, were stripped of the title 'Inlander,' and banished to the unexplored regions east of Innerland. They were further warned that the next penalty would be death on sight if any of them, or their followers, were ever seen by an Inlander again. I did say four individuals were banished, didn't I? Well, I guess maybe Jori's vote didn't count after all.

-CHAPTER TWENTY-ONE-
Endings

The varied collection of people, animals, and goods, had all arrived to Outside. Finally. Considering the numbers of people, the exodus from Innerland had been accomplished with surprising speed and organization. It had occurred within about a month's time. Even so, it seemed to take forever, and I don't remember working so hard before in my entire life. Though Gamious had thought to rule over all of Innerland, it was apparent that the real structure which held the people together was that which had been in place for ages; the Council of the Ancients. It had been my idea to come here, but the Inlanders, working together, had been the ones who had given life to my thought.

Gamious' armed forces hadn't put up much of a fight when they heard that their leader was in captivity. Many of his guards had been conscripted originally anyway, and so were relieved to renounce Gamious and be let out of servitude to him.

Some of the Gamious' chief leaders, however, were die-hards. They accompanied their master even on his journey of banishment to the unexplored regions east of Innerland, past the wilderness areas of Outland. Gamious, and those who still followed him, were made to leave occupied Innerland before the populace journeyed to Outside. Tabob and Ker-Lee (the new Head Guards) trailed Gamious and crew for two days. They took a large contingent of men to make certain those in exile went away. No one wanted Gamious to know where Outside was. Four days after the banishment Tabob and Ker-Lee returned. The people began their preparations for journeying to a new home, far from generations of familiarity with Innerland.

The gold? The Ancients realized that the strange shiny metal had wielded an unholy power on Gamious, and had turned him from being their political leader, into a power-crazed despot. Most of the Ancients, wisely, wanted nothing to do with it. However, the pictures of the countryside that came from Gamious' private chamber were taken along so that the people might remember the beauty that had once been Innerland.

Mib regained consciousness our second day in Outside. Vocata had set up his family home near the burial chamber of my mother. It seemed an appropriate home-site, as it had once been the ancestral home of my mother's people before they journeyed to Innerland. I was fortunate enough to be keeping watch over Mib when she awoke. Her bed had been moved into the protective half-shade of the trees near Vocata's new dwelling. I watched as Mib squinted briefly up at the sun as it peeked through the foliage. I looked up too, and noted that the position of the sun had changed slightly from when I had first seen it, eight cycles before. Then Mib quietly asked, "Jeff, is that a... star?"

"Yes, it is," I replied, startled, but happy to hear her speak. I shaded her eyes with my hand. "But don't look at it too long or it will hurt your vision," I quickly added.

Still squinting her eyes, she looked away and said, "I must be dreaming..."

"It's real, buddy," I assured her as I reached down to hold her hand.

I called for her family. Tabob, her parents, and I embraced her simultaneously. Pounce, who hadn't left her side for very long during the past several weeks, screeched and took temporary refuge in the tree-tops to escape the sudden crush of humans.

I continued living with Vocata and his family for several more months. My memories of the time with my brother's family are some of the happiest I possess. One morning though, I awoke with a feeling I'd not remembered dealing with before. Like the fear I had felt around Gamious, it was strange to me. But I didn't feel fear now. I was homesick. Homesick for my father, and the family that, although perhaps not typical, was my family. I knew then that I would leave my newfound friends, my new family. When I told Vocata of my decision at breakfast, he persuaded me to remain for another few days, so that I might address the people before I left, and give to them a name. I reluctantly agreed; *I hate long farewells.*

The time came for me to give a final address. The people gathered in a huge amphitheater carved from solid rock. Vocata told me I would not even have to raise my voice much to be heard by all of those assembled. Not all of the people had come, I'm sure, but at that moment, standing before more people than I had ever seen, it felt like I stood before the whole of Innerland. I clutched the talisman beneath my shirt for strength. It felt cold to my touch. I knew somehow, that whatever came out of me next, had to be from inside of me; I would receive no magical help in my speech.

I stood then, on the podium, knowing that it would probably be the last time that I might see some of the people that had, over the last months, become so important to me. What added to the joy I then felt, as I stood, contemplating the vast multitude gathered before me, was the knowledge that I had actually done something worthwhile for each of them. I had shown them a bounteous world where they and their families could live and thrive, instead of being stuck in the squalor that Gamious had reduced Innerland to. What most people thought to be fancy and imagination a few months ago, had been revealed as a world where they, and their families, could live and flourish for generations to come. What could I possibly say?

I took a deep breath, and just as I had discovered my purpose as a Deliverer, the right words and commitments then came to me as I stood before the assemblage of Inlanders to speak. "I leave you now, in the wise care and keeping of Vocata, my brother, and the other Ancients. I go to my world to study, and to be with my family. I know what I will study the next several years of my life. I will learn about how to care for and manage the environment. I will return as I am able, and as I learn I will share my learning.

Each of you should also use your time wisely. Become familiar with your new world. Learn how to use it, but also how to care for it. Think how you might repair the damage that the servants of Gamious did to Innerland. Perhaps then, when I return, we can work out a balance between using the worlds of Outside and Innerland. Both could be used, with neither being wasted. In that day, as we both come to greater knowledge and wisdom, perhaps you will be able to depend less on a Deliverer like myself, and more on your own people, and the dreams that will come from you and your children.

"I would never want the conduit between our worlds closed, however. There seems to be some deeper purpose in the exchange that has taken place between us than just what might be learned about the environment. Our worlds, though different, are connected now in a way that they have never been. Blood of Innerland flows in my world, from my mother through me. Blood of my world now flows through Innerland by way of Vocata and his family. Perhaps the time shift can be understood and better controlled so that our visits may be better planned and more regular. Some of you may see me again; I will try not to let three hundred cycles pass before my return. Take care of this second chance you have been given."

Stepping off of the podium, I walked to a great tree and placed my hand upon the vole of it. "Innerland was a single tree. Though great in size, it had an end when enough of you took food and shelter from it. Plant more trees to replace the ones you use. Give to your world as well as take, and you will all live long on this land you have been given." I plucked a seedpod from an overhanging branch, and placed it into the eager hand of a bright-eyed little girl.

"One last thing. Vocata has told me that it was up to me to name this people, as all Deliverer's have done before me. The name that your ancestors had who lived Outside was Terrainian. You, though, have been called Inlanders since your migration to Innerland, hundreds of cycles ago. I think upon the beauty that was Innerland, and could be again. I would not take that beauty away from you. Innerland nurtured you and allowed you to grow. Because you have been in Innerland, Innerland will always be in you. Keep Innerland in your hearts. I now name this people, a name that they might retain the memory of Innerland always in their hearts. You will continue from this time forth, to be Inlanders; I now declare it, as your Deliverer." The cheers from those assembled precluded my saying anything else. I think I had said what was needed.

Completing my farewell to the people, I looked around once more at the vast forests, teeming with life that stretched in every direction beyond my line of sight. As I stepped down, I turned to Vocata and his family.

Pounce stayed with Mib. It was his home, but it was nearly as difficult to say goodbye to that little green rodent, as it was to say goodbye to Mib, or the others. Vocata and I returned the artifacts that Iamb had given me to my mother's tomb. I felt they should be there for the next Deliverer. I had, however, added my history of my own experiences to the words my father had written when it was his turn. I found those last months that I really liked writing, almost as much as drawing. But I also embellished my history with pictures. I was, after all, still planning to illustrate comics as an aside.

The transition back to my world was accomplished after a tear filled farewell with my little brother; the old man named Vocata. I knew I probably wouldn't get to see him again in this life. But at least I had the chance to meet my brother, whom I had never before known.

* * *

After my return, Dad and I stayed up until early Sunday morning. He listened eagerly to every detail as I recounted my experiences in Innerland. After I finished, we sat for long moments. Then he spoke, and broke the silence.

"Then it's over... For now."

"For now," I emphasized. "But I have promised to return after going to college, to teach the Inlanders to manage their environment. I'll need your help with that."

"We'll cross that bridge when it comes, Son. Right now, you'd better get some sleep so you can finish your homework later. See you in the morning," he said as he got up to go to bed.

"Dad? It is morning," I said as I pointed to the clock. We both laughed. His laughter sounded like Vocata's laughter. It was a sound I had not heard in a long time. It felt good to hear it. It reminded me of how families must feel. Then I approached my dad with an idea that had been bugging me since my final, nearly fatal, conflict with Gamious.

"Dad. The Stone of Recognition can reverse time. I only made it go back a moment, as you'll remember from my story, but maybe we could learn how to get time to go back further. You could see them both again." I offered. He stopped and looked at me. I wasn't certain of the emotion he was feeling. "You could tell Mom that you didn't desert her," I continued, "You could live out the life with her that you were meant to live, the life you missed."

After staring at me for what seemed an eternity, he smiled and said, "Time is a fickle thing, Jeff. Perhaps I might satisfy my personal need to undo a regret... but at what cost? Would you have to re-do everything that you've worked so hard to accomplish with the migration of the Inlanders these past months? Would the second run through time give the evil faction of Gamious another chance to turn the tide in their favor? Could I really bring back the dead? We have both been given a special power for some reason, but neither of us can claim to have the power of the Gods. Besides..."

His voice trailed off, then Dad got a faraway look in his eyes, and was silent for a moment. In a choked voice he continued, "Your mom knows that I didn't desert her, Jeff. I saw her last night. She came to me... I talked with her, and told her I had tried to come back. Told her one last time that I loved her. Held her hand even. I think that she really visited me somehow, that it wasn't just a dream. Jeff, I know this sounds crazy, and I can't explain it logically, but I don't think dreams feel that real, I-"

I rushed forward with my arms wide and cut him off mid-sentence. We stood there, the two of us, embracing for long moments. There was between us then, a communication of feeling even more powerful than the power Iamb exercised when he put thoughts in my mind while teaching me. As our arms let go their grip around each other, my dad held me firmly by my shoulders. An understanding look passed between us, stronger than anything communicated by words. For the first time in a long while I knew of Dad's love for me, and I believe that he knew of my love for him.

In a way that weekend, Dad and I both got something we each needed, and I think, even wanted. I am beginning to see that reality can hold adventure bigger and more exciting than anything contained even in a Captain Amazing comic book. And Dad? Well, I believe he is learning to dream once again.

-EPILOGUE-
Beginnings

Dad was helpful in assisting me to outline my goals for the future. We ended up staying up late Sunday talking about our ideas while I worked on my homework. I know college is a long ways off yet, but having a plan, rather than just sailing through life, seems a more intelligent approach to what lies ahead; I had at least learned that from Innerland. So it looks as though science will be my area of study. I never pictured myself as a scientist, but I am willing to learn. One thing I will need to improve is my ability to do mathematics. But I have a commitment to keep, so I will find a way through it. I'm keeping the art too; it's something I already do well, and just might add to my ability to communicate ideas in science. Besides, it's a lot of fun.

I was back in school today, and things felt pretty much normal. Nicer, really. I have goals to do better. I know, I know, I've said it before. But this time, somehow, I believe it will be different. I just have a feeling. I think it has something to do with the fact that it is *my goal* this time… not Dad's, or Mrs. Weshey's, or anyone else's goal. *Mine*.

My time in Innerland gave me a real chance to grow. I know, I know—I still look the same on the outside. It's because the time differential between our worlds caused my physical body to stay about the same. But I feel older, inside. Heck, I got to experience several months in the time that everybody else spent part of a normal weekend. In the time that some of my peers watched cartoons, or went to the mall, I managed to help save Innerland, and still got most of my homework finished. I wonder what I'll do next weekend?

I confess that not all of my homework was done, but I was better prepared for school Monday morning than I had been in awhile. (It still blows my mind to think that everything happened pretty much overnight from the perspective of our world!) Anyway, my teachers were pleased. I was pleased too. I'm sticking with my plans to do better in school. This time I think I have the motivation to really make the change, due in part to some events that took place this afternoon.

At lunchtime I was off by myself with my sketchpad, doing some drawings of Innerland; partly for my own benefit (because I felt a little homesick) and partially because my sketchbook was due this afternoon in Mrs. Tistry's art class. From my experiences during the 'weekend' I also had plans for a killer creative writing assignment that I had received in Mr. Engold's class second hour. Nobody would believe my story was true anyway, so I would bill it as a creative writing effort. Caught up in my drawing, and how I might write my story, I was suddenly startled by an unfamiliar voice.

"Those are nice. You've got quite an imagination, Jeff." ...*A girl's voice?*

I turned around slowly. Standing in front of me was a student my age, shoulder length brown hair, real attractive.

"Sorry to interrupt you. My name's Jana." She held out her hand to shake mine, and then continued, "I'm in your math class, fourth hour. My mom and I just moved here about three weeks ago."

I remembered her. I had noticed her in my math class that day, as I had about every day for the last couple of weeks. I recall thinking that as good looking as she was, there would be no chance that I would ever get to meet her because she would soon be hanging around with the 'in' crowd. But come to think of it, I hadn't seen her hanging around with that group.

"Where do you get the ideas for such fantastic landscape and creatures?" she asked as she sat down beside me. She seemed genuinely interested. No one besides Mrs. Tistry and Mib had ever taken interest in my drawings before. It felt nice to have the interest.

"Well, my dad says I have an active imagination," I replied. "Do you like drawing?" I asked her.

"Like it, yes. But I'm no good at it," she replied.

"That's nonsense," I countered, "Anyone can draw! It's like a game. You just have to know what shapes to look for, and how to show it on paper."

"That's what Mr. Measer says about math. That it's just a game that anyone can learn as long as that person understands the rules."

"You've been talking to Mr. Measer about math too, huh? He has neat ideas," I replied. "In fact, I have regular visits with him myself... about how poorly I am doing in his class. I am trying harder these days though. Do you have those kind of visits too?" I asked.

"Actually, no." Jana answered. "He says that I have a 'keen understanding for a student my age'." Jana laughed, and I did too, especially at the way she imitated his constantly firm yet nasal tone. "That's why I came to see you," she continued, "Mr. Measer said you weren't doing so well in his class and asked me if I would be willing to help you. He really believes you can succeed, but just doesn't know how to help you. He thought maybe I could."

"Oh." I replied flatly, and turned back to my drawing. I wanted to do better in school, but I wasn't interested in anyone patronizing me.

Ignoring my rudeness, Jana continued talking to me. "I told him that I would try to help you in math, Jeff. But not just because he asked me to," she hastily added. "I wanted to. I haven't really made too many friends yet, and I've wanted to meet you since I saw your superhero drawings hanging by the office during the art contest last week. I've even heard some of the kids talking about the silkscreen shirts you've designed. In fact, there goes one now, " she said as she pointed to a kid who'd bought one from me at the art fair.

I turned back around. At least this lady had good taste in art.

"I hope I didn't make you feel badly," she continued, "But I wanted to be honest up front. That way if you were mad, you wouldn't have to waste time becoming friends with me. I believe in being honest, Jeff"

Friends? Cool! I thought, trying to hide my growing smile.

"I believe in being honest too, Jana. Mr. Measer was being nice when he said I wasn't doing very well in math. To be honest, I'm actually dying in math!" I confessed as I let part of my smile show. "I could really use some help, if you're willing. I want to go into science, but the math really gets in my way. I even want to learn, but I can't pay much money for tutoring or anything."

She laughed. "Well, since we're confessing here, I also have a confession to make," Jana said with a smirk.

"I'm listening," I replied, with an imitation look of smugness. I put down my drawing pad and folded my arms across my chest.

"Well. I know it's not a big deal if I flunk art or not, but to me it is. And I'm pretty much failing. Even though I try, I can't seem to make my drawings look like anything. I have problems even with stick people, and I think Mrs. Tistry has given up on me. I'd really like to draw like you do, Jeff."

I couldn't believe this was happening. Me, talking to a girl who actually wanted to talk with me! It was more amazing to me than anything I'd seen in Innerland, or even read in Captain Amazing. Besides, it felt really good to be talking to a girl like this.

"Maybe we could trade expertise, Jana," I suggested.

Jana smiled, and replied, "I was hoping you'd say that, Jeff."

Well, Jana and I spent the rest of the lunch hour visiting. She didn't seem as superficial as some of the 'popular' crowd I had pegged her likely to hang around. I was amazed that someone that liked math and I had so much in common.

After school, I walked her home. The warm spring air felt nice. I felt as alive as the newly renewed trees as Jana and I walked and visited. We stopped to watch some squirrels playing in a giant elm tree. Seeing their aerial acrobatics caused me to miss Pounce, but I believed he was probably better off in his own world with Mib.

Well, I've got to go now. You see, Jana invited me over to have dinner with her and her mom. Jana assures me that her two little sisters will be there to tease me too. I've got to go get ready. Afterwards, Jana's going to help me study the math homework for tomorrow's class. I might even help her with the design project for Mrs. Tistry's class. With what has happened to me in the last couple of days, I'm beginning to think that our world may not be as bad as I first thought when finally coming back from Innerland. See you around. Oh, one last thing: don't listen to anybody that makes fun of your dreams—trust yourself, and go make your dreams a reality.

—Jeffrey Ransford: Artist, Student, Dreamer… and Deliverer

Made in the USA
San Bernardino, CA
15 August 2015